tell her everything

Mirza Waheed was born and brought up in Kashmir. His debut novel, *The Collaborator,* was an international bestseller, a finalist for the Guardian First Book Award and the Shakti Bhatt Prize, and longlisted for the Desmond Elliott Prize. It was also a book of the year for *The Telegraph, New Statesman, Financial Times, Business Standard* and *The Telegraph* (India), among others.

His novel, *The Book of Gold Leaves,* was published in 2014 to critical acclaim. It was shortlisted for the DSC Prize for South Asian Literature 2016, longlisted for the Folio Prize and was a finalist at the 2015 Tata Literature Live! Book of the Year (Fiction).

Mirza has written for the BBC, *The Guardian, Granta, Guernica, Al Jazeera* (English) and *The New York Times.*

Praise for *Tell Her Everything*

'A brilliant, unsettling and sometimes horrifying novel. How, it asks, does the unconscionable become everyday—or, as the narrator asks, how does the abnormal become normal? Dr K is a superb creation, a narrator of unreliable morality. Kafka and Coetzee come to mind, of course, but also Ishiguro's *Never Let Me Go*; this has the same unheimlich shudder, the same sense of tapping into deeply repressed fears.'

—Alex Preston

'It's really quite extraordinary. The story of how small men become party to huge crimes is so important. This is a powerful, profound and important novel—one that has really sunk into my imagination in a way that too little does these days.'

—Kamila Shamsie

'Mirza Waheed's new novel is an eloquent and powerful testament to the fragility of our moral codes—and especially resonant at a time when those codes are being violated like never before.'

—Pankaj Mishra

Reviews of *Tell Her Everything*

A BuzzFeed Most Anticipated Thriller of 2023

'Waheed's novels function a bit like the glass backing of a watch that allows you to glimpse inside its mechanics; only in this case, behind the crystal glass, you can see the cogs of his characters' guilty consciences whirring. As we read about them in their studied transparency, we realise that these are consciences that might have been any of ours, confronted with the prospect of treachery and collusion in the wrong place at the wrong time.'

—Tanjil Rashid, *The Guardian*

'Waheed's work comes at a time when we have pushed the bar lower and lower about what we can say and do with impunity. This is a simple yet powerful book in itself, but the rudderlessness of these times makes it resonate with an even deeper urgency.'

—Vaishna Roy, *The Hindu*

'In Mirza Waheed's delicately layered new novel, a retired doctor recounts his life's circumstances and choices, presenting a desperate portrait of unrelenting guilt ... a sedate exploration of moral accountability, of the ethics and emotions of morality.'

—Saudamini Jain, *Hindustan Times*

'At first glance, Shah's tale seems like it will follow the route of the typical Indian immigrant success story. But Waheed does something different with his third novel, narrated mostly as a story told by Shah to his daughter. He melds Mohammed Hanif's narrative style and Julian Barnes' literary flourish to warp this trope into one about trauma and complicity in institutionalised violence.'

—Karthik Shankar, *Huffington Post*

'The confession of the source of his unease comes together gradually, like pieces of a jigsaw puzzle that stubbornly resist falling into place for a long time. But when it is finally revealed, the enormity of our insight into his Dr Jekyll and Mr Hyde persona is momentous, darkening the mood of what had felt like the opening act of a sentimental domestic drama.'

—Somak Ghoshal, *Mint*

'Waheed's debut novel, *The Collaborator*, also featured a first-person account, one set in Kashmir, with the narrator bedevilled by thoughts of a subversive alliance with the Indian security forces. *Tell Her Everything* is another report by a collaborator, and in its refusal to be black or white, it affirms that we're all many shades of grey.'

—Sanjay Sipahimalani, *Scroll*

'[A] layered recital of intricately woven hauntings, decisions, and confessions ... This novel presents a series of moral complexities but doesn't attempt to offer clear answers or settle for easy resolutions—the disquietude is central to its effectiveness ... at once haunting, tender, and gripping.

—Farooq Chaudhry, *Chicago Review of Books*

'The horror and beauty of *Tell Her Everything* essentially deals with the moral choices a person makes in modern times. It's a story ... addressed to the reader, making him/her an intimate participant.'

—Aradhika Sharma, *The Tribune* (India)

'Mirza Waheed speaks of a blunt, ubiquitous truth: society's quest for global dominion and its inevitable trajectory towards the immoral and corrupt in pursuit of the said goal ... What appears to be the story of a strained father-daughter relationship also depicts at a more fundamental level the "moral exhaustion" of one man, father, husband and doctor who discovers just how much he has corrupted his soul in chasing after his ambitions.'

—Aishwarya Sahasrabudhe, *FirstPost*

'As he tells it, he was an ordinary man caught up in unexpected, extraordinary circumstances ... Evil became mundane in his world while love grew distant ... a novel about how the choices we make affect those we love in ways we could never imagine.'

—*Foreword Reviews*

MIRZA WAHEED
tell her everything
a novel

cntxt

First published in hardback by Context, an imprint of Westland Publications Private Limited, in 2018

First published in paperback by Context, an imprint of Westland Books, a division of Nasadiya Technologies Private Limited, in 2023

No. 269/2B, First Floor, 'Irai Arul', Vimalraj Street, Nethaji Nagar, Alapakkam Main Road, Maduravoyal, Chennai 600095

ISBN: 9789357767996

10 9 8 7 6 5 4 3 2 1

Typeset by SÜRYA, New Delhi
Printed at Manipal Technologies Limited, Manipal

'It is not by confining one's neighbour that one is convinced of one's own sanity.'

– Fyodor Dostoyevsky,
Diary of a Writer

'To write prescriptions is easy, but to come to an understanding with people is hard.'

– Franz Kafka,
A Country Doctor

PART I

1

I DID IT FOR MONEY.

I'll tell her. She may or may not understand, but I've decided to tell her everything, the whole truth, as straight as possible.

In fact, I don't think anyone can fully understand. It's not really understandable that I spent more than two decades in that town and I didn't know the townspeople. Was it a town or a proper city, I do not know for sure. How do I explain to people that I, a grown man, not wholly unsociable, spent most of my time, over twenty years, between my home and the hospital? And home was less than a mile away. How do I explain that I lived in that mile for years without really getting to know the local people or cuisine, or what customs existed among those people? The reason is this: I lived from procedure to procedure, from case to case. That's what.

—

There was just one tree on the street, at the lower end where the hospital compound ended. Sometimes I stopped beside it. Its bark was the colour of cement.

When I arrived there all those years ago, it was almost always hot. Even when it was not. A small gap in the cold shield created by countless AC vents sometimes let in a quick reminder of the heat. Of how hot it really was. After about eight years or so, I began to feel cold. It's the truth, Sara, I'll tell her. All those cold draughts had probably crept into my marrow over the years. That lasted a few years too, during which I wore a light leather jacket—you might remember. You were four or five then.

In those early days, I had quite a lot of time on my hands. It took five minutes to reach the hospital, ten if I walked, which I often did. No one else walked, apart from the cleaning staff, Jan and the others, who lived in concrete cabins at the edge of the compound. They walked or pushed their trolleys. I looked at them and wondered if this was the colour of their skin or a consequence of having worked in these parts for years. Every time I saw any of them, I wanted to make sure they had a large wet towel around their neck. I was glad when they did.

There wasn't much to do after work—you weren't born yet—so Atiya and I watched a lot of TV. A lot of good and bad TV. Chinese, Malaysian, Turkish, and Indian films with subtitles. If you think Bollywood is melodramatic, you need to watch Turkish films from the Eighties. There was nothing else to do. There were no cinemas in the area. None at all. Yes, there were a few restaurants by the canal on the other side of the town, my colleague and only friend Biju said, but they were very expensive. Actually, money wasn't the issue, they were just too far away and I was afraid of taking Atiya out for long. I'll explain later. Many years later, when I finally ate at two of them, I was glad I hadn't taken her. The canal smelled of bleach. I didn't trust it.

~

My friend Biju, single, with no obligations back home in Kerala, spent a lot on eating out. Almost every day after work, he went in search of a good meal and sometimes returned home having had two dinners. 'I can't go to bed with a disappointing taste in my mouth. It's against my principles,' he said. 'You should join me some day, boss ... Okay, at least come along to Gold City when I go next.' Every month, usually on the first weekend after payday, Biju would disappear. Only after we had him over for dinner a couple of times did he say he went to Dubai to eat at expensive restaurants. 'Say whatever about the city, boss, but you can eat, buy, do anything and everything you want. I had this Japanese beef curry and Japanese beer, and I just didn't want to leave, boss.'

I knew Biju went to get drunk but I didn't tell anyone. I liked him. I also knew he had worked out some kind of arrangement with the admin people, who frequently let him slip in and out.

~

The first year went very quickly. We bought quite a few appliances and a brand new Pajero, which was the main reason I preferred to walk, despite the heat. After a while,

I mean after the initial excitement, it felt silly to start such a large car, get it out of the garage, which wasn't easy because of the clutter the previous owners had left, and then drive for a mere five minutes.

You see, Sara—I'll definitely say this to her—it's only now, with the knowledge that comes with age and experience, that I can say I'm pleased I left in the end. While I was there, I didn't have the benefit of distance to look at things with clarity. Certainly not at the beginning. Of course I had the wisdom to make sure you left early. But what I, you, *we*, lost over there can never be fully understood, let alone recovered. We only have each other now, and I hope you understand that. Of course you do, of course you do. Why would I ever doubt that?

Before I lay it all out, before I recount everything, I should appeal to her heart; bring her closer to me. It might even be time to have a drink with her. That would be grand, wouldn't it? We'll sit here in the balcony, savour the breeze from the river, and I'll tell her everything. Every single thing. We'll look at the lights of this glorious, saddening old city, and talk. I'll point out the new skyscrapers to her. She might like them. Many people in the city aren't too fond of the towers and call them all sorts of names. What about you, she might ask? I'm sure she will. Oh, I don't mind them. Lights in the sky, lights in the distance, are always welcome. They add colour to the big smoke at night. I don't get what people have against tall buildings. Do they worry that the skyscrapers will spoil their view of a clear and blue sky, eh? I'm sure you like them, Sara, you must be used to them ... Yeah, I don't mind them, Dad.

I mean I don't notice them much. In America, we don't, like, go on about skyscrapers much, you know. They're just there, she'll say, and probably smile.

Sara has Atiya's smile, a slight upward curve to the left of her upper lip. So tiny, only I can spot it. Of course only I can spot it. I doubt anyone else remembers Atiya's smile so minutely.

I think I'll tell her about those early days first, about the hospital, my work, about Sir Farhad, about Biju, other colleagues, etcetera. We can surely have an ordinary conversation before I move on to the other stuff. I must tell her. This year, I am ready at last and I'm sure she is too. She should know the whole thing. I hope she isn't too upset. Why would she feel upset with a story about her mother and father! I think she'll like to stretch out on the settee, or perhaps relax in my rocking chair, and admire the views across the river. I'll cook for her, and I'll look at her every now and then from the kitchen.

2

AT WORK, I ALWAYS STARTED the day with a large coffee. It was free and very good coffee, made lovingly by the machine attendant. Zoheb loved his work, anyone could tell from the way he wiped the smallest drop from the steel frame. He was from Sylhet, in Bangladesh, but left the country soon after completing a diploma in mechanical engineering, he said. Biju, always quick to pounce on a poor joke, called him Barista Bengali. Like me, Zoheb was a double migrant. While I'd just moved from London, he had, until a couple of years ago, worked in a vast bakery in Rome, making pyramids of croissants from midnight, he said. 'I worked six days, Dr Saab, six days, often doing double shifts, didn't see a lot of daylight or of Rome. Here they pay me more than twice for half the work! And I was sick of eating misshapen croissants for lunch and dinner five days a week.'

Of course, here, I mean over there, he had to keep his head down at all times, something he didn't mention. But I felt he was genuinely grateful. I knew I was.

—

You see, Sara, you may not be able to appreciate this fully. I come from what's sometimes called a humble background. It's shorthand for low income. My parents were poor. For someone like me, then, it's a life-changing moment when income exceeds expenditure for the first time. Yes, that's exactly the way I want to put it. You begin to think and act differently. The shoulders, tense for a lifetime, suddenly lose the grip of that coil inside. You don't have to worry about a shortfall, about borrowing more, or how to avoid a creditor. The first time is just delicious, even life affirming, if I may say so. Your back relaxes. In less than three months of working in Sir Farhad's hospital, we had extra cash in the bank account—can you believe that? Atiya and I actually hugged. I had tears in my eyes but I didn't cry. And it is to that moment, when I became aware of the possibility of saving money, making it grow actually, that I owe everything. You think this apartment would've been possible had I not worked over there?

We have moved from relative poverty to being a high-income household within my lifetime. Don't you find that remarkable? I do. You'll inherit abundance, my dear, not dearth. You'll be free, not tied to your parents' debts and dignity.

You probably don't even remember how much your school fees were. When I was a teenager, I wrote letters for our rich relatives so that I could pay my own fees. I didn't want it to be a drain on our limited income. My father, may he rest in heaven, used to write letters to supplement his income, so one day I said, 'Abbu, I can do a few too, for pocket money, that's all.' He didn't say no. It was the most laborious way to earn money; some part-time trade, like selling socks and undergarments (hosiery, I mean) door to door, would've brought more money for much less work. But reading and writing was all we knew, Sara.

Uff, more than forty-two years have passed since those days, but I remember everything. Would you like to hear about it?

One day, Abbu and I sat in our relative's showy living room—they had no taste whatsoever—writing his business and personal correspondence. I was seventeen, I think. The family owned and ran shops in Muscat, and exported brassware from Muradabad. As I sat there writing 'Thanking You in Anticipation' and 'Yours Sincerely', I couldn't help looking through the sliding door that led to the dining room. They sat at a long glass table, eating, chatting, laughing, while my father and I drank tea and ate biscuits. Why do I remember that day more than the others, Sara? Why? Take a guess ... Because that moment told me I had to cover the distance from our table to the other side and become those people. With better taste, of course.

No! I didn't take an oath, nothing dramatic like that, my dear. Come on. I simply understood something. Maybe it had something to do with the look of discomfort or shame on my father's face. (I really don't know how to describe it.) Or maybe my own sense of a humiliation that I shouldn't have felt. What I remember clearly is thinking, 'No. This is not the life I want to live. This is not the life I want to hand down to my children.'

What were the letters like, Dad? I mean, you know, like, what did you have to write?

I know Sara won't be able to resist. She does have something of her mother's sense of humour, after all.

Oh, classic desi stuff, dear: sentimental, a bit over the top, as they say nowadays, O-T-T, isn't it? *I hope this letter of mine finds you in the best of health and wealth and I beseech the Almighty to bless you with everything you wish for, both in this world and in the hereafter.*

Come on, Dad, they didn't really say best of wealth, did they?

Yes, they really did. Wait, there's more. A few years later, Abbu said his cousin had quietly asked him to write letters to his second wife or mistress whom he had hidden away in Muscat. I'd just graduated and was on an intern's stipend at the local government hospital. My father wasn't one to talk much about such matters, but when I joked and moaned about those awful letters, he burst out: 'Mister, you had it easy. I was writing "my daaarrling, the love of my life, my truest wife, I miss you more than ever, your absence is like a cold knife in my side ..." to some poor woman in another part of the world. Sometimes, that sinner, may he rot in hell, asked me to write nice stuff on my own. I had to invent endearments for a secret wife on behalf of my unlettered cousin.'

~

Almost every evening, as I walk in the balcony, looking at the river below, the lights on the opposite bank, buses and cars that crawl like glow worms on the Waterloo bridge, I recall the kind of satisfaction and, how do I describe it—worrylessness?—Atiya and I felt that day, all those years ago, in our house over there.

How I miss her, how I wish I could share this moment, this light that spreads over me every evening, with her. This I had dreamt of, to retire and come back to London with her. Atiya would probably not approve of the wine, but she wasn't so narrow-minded as to ask me to stop. I seriously doubt it. The void she left, as I said, keeps growing. I don't fight it, I never have.

3

It's a clear, fog-free evening. Tourist boats cruise on the river. I like looking at them as they glide through the muddy water. Like brightly lit whales with people inside them, I sometimes think. Not all are tourist boats. Some are party floats, where people eat, drink and dance. Sitting here, on my own sky deck, I sometimes play a game: I count the number of people on a boat deck before it escapes my field of vision. A few times, I've had to rush to the edge of the balcony to notch up the last few shadows.

When Sara has rested a day or two, I'll ask her if she'd like to sit in the balcony with me. I hope she does. It's not too cold. Only October, and the chill factor hasn't arrived yet.

Even if it makes her uncomfortable, I'll tell her the whole story. I worry that if I die now, no one will ever know about my journey; my life story, so to speak. I don't mean everyone needs to know, but my daughter certainly does. I sent her away, half of my heart with her, and there's a lot that happened before and after that she simply doesn't know. Now, she must.

Yes, I don't want her to spend the best years of her life piecing together the story of her parents. Might as well put it all together before I'm gone. It's all in my head, bristling through the synapses.

And I've thought this through over the years. I've gone through cycles of doubt, boredom and loathing. I have mulled it over and over again. I've relived so many moments, evening after evening, year after year. And these last few years, I've waited for Sara. I've looked at the murmurous Thames below me and trailed its waters to the ocean beyond the city, vast and foreboding, yes, but easily bested by a quick flight. That's all it'll take, a single flight, I've told myself on mornings and evenings, as I've waited for her to grow old enough to be able to listen to what I have to say. Now really is the time.

I'm certain she'll come. We are not estranged, far from it. It's just that she's been busy, tied up, making a life of her own. Nothing, absolutely nothing, gives me more satisfaction than that single concrete fact. A life of her own. These are, after all, the most crucial years for her. She hasn't visited for quite some time but I've been patient. Wonder if she feels guilty. I don't want her to. She doesn't know that a large part of me might have wanted it this way. I wasn't ready, and I did the right thing to protect her.

You were fourteen or fifteen then, what could I have said to you, Sara? I'll say to her.

So you had a sense I knew something, Dad, didn't you? she may retort.

How do you know, how *can* you know? I'm afraid this is pure conjecture on your part. You don't know. Even I don't know.

Sara probably doesn't remember that, when I asked

to meet her then (I was even looking at tickets), she'd said, yes, 'but not now, Dad, you'd agree it's a big thing … I want to come properly when I'm ready, I can't take it lightly'. This is more or less the crux of what she said.

Oh, I have missed her like I've never missed anything. After Atiya, that is. Now, I'm ready and I think she is too. I'll explain everything and she'll understand everything. There is, there must still be, love between us.

~

I want to tell her this, for instance.

I know some of our relatives hated me when I sent you to boarding school, Sara. Your uncle Aqil in particular. I never really understood his disapproval. I know he probably blamed his sister's death on me—which was hurtful to say the very least—so shouldn't he have been pleased that I sent you away? In those days, I sometimes wished his wife would die, too, you know, so he would understand what it was like. Loose, angry words get stuck in the heart like a thorn under the nail. How could I tell them that it had nothing to do with your mother's passing? Not one person tried to understand how hard, how crushing, it was for me to first lose Atiya and then to have to send you away. Not one. How could I keep you with me, while doing the work I did? How? It was different when you were a child, but as you grew up, and you were such a clever little girl, I worried what effect it might have on you.

I had to send you away, Sara, I had to.

If one relative from your mom's side, or from my side

for that matter, had tried to understand that I had my reasons, or the simple fact that no father sends his only child away soon after his wife's death unless it's necessary, I wouldn't have snapped ties with them. What am I saying? They cut off ties with me, and I just let it stay that way. Biju also said there was nothing I could do about it, so I just let it be.

Of course Aqil has been very good to you. Why wouldn't he be? I wish I'd been able to visit you as he did in those days. But I swear I don't hold that against you. I have resented him over the years, I admit, but never you. Come on, you're my daughter, my only family. And, overall, I have spent more time with you than he has. I've got that on him, don't I; he can't compete on that count, not if I include the childhood years?

The greatest irony of all is that, after Atiya died, it became more difficult for me to leave the job. Even as it gradually became clear to me that it was taking a toll on me ... on my sanity, fuck it. But with you in boarding school, I just didn't want to take a risk. How could I? I had to remain worry-free on your account. Every month, as I put a part of the salary into your account, it became clearer that I couldn't take a chance with your future. No, please, please, don't even remotely think that I'm trying to put it all on you. I'm just trying to explain how it was in those days.

Of course I remember the first time, how can I forget? But, you see, as with most first times, you don't really know it's the beginning of something. And when I did, I just couldn't extricate myself. Or maybe I didn't want to. You were adjusting well to your new life.

The only bit of wisdom I've gained, or think I've gained, over the years is that clarity isn't possible, and seeking it is always going to be, how do I say ... fraught!

[I should avoid the 'F' word in front of her. Yes. I don't want her to think her father has turned into one of those foul-mouthed, bitter old men who can't keep their tongue in check.]

I was right to have sent you away from myself, Sara, from your mother's memory, from the place where it all happened. I wept when I read your first letter. I must've probably cried more then than I did when you left, or when Atiya left us—may she rest in Jannat-ul-Firdaus. It was pathetic, I admit, breaking down like that, all by myself on the sofa. But the next day, I went to work and got busy.

4

Just like in England—in the two years I worked here in the late Eighties, that is, and I don't know what it's like now—all the bosses over there were natives. Some nice, some rude, some indifferent. During the first year itself, I sensed that many of the rumours about those people, about that place, were exaggerations or simply untrue. Stereotypes, really.

In my very first week at work, the director of the hospital, Sir Farhad, invited me to his office and offered tea and biscuits. They were Belgian biscuits, I remember because I saw the tin. The sofa in his office was almost as big as our living room. The office half a football ground. I envied him.

'In my hospital there's only one rule. Work hard and treat the patients with respect. If you do everything that's expected of you, the hospital will look after you. It's that simple. You must also remember, if the director sends some people to you, it means they're important people. You have to treat them as top priority. Sometimes they'll have nothing. You'll find there's no illness apart from vague or angry complaints, but you must always treat them well and with respect.'

'I will, sir. And, forgive me, what shall I do if I'm … attending to an emergency case … Sir Farhad?'

'Still try to be nice. Of course you mustn't let anyone die because you're attending to the director's nephew. But still try to be nice.'

'I'll do my maximum best. I'll work very hard,' I said.

He then turned to his giant computer, and I finished my tea in silence.

—

At first, I worked in a sub-team in Emergency with two other doctors, both imported like me. One of them, Abdel Hamad, was from Lebanon and the other, Sujo, was from the Philippines. I didn't even know there were Muslims in the Philippines. They didn't talk to me much for the first three or four months. I was the new guy and they were senior to me.

And, like I said, there was only the one friend I made over there, Biju, Biju Thomas Tharakan, the anaesthetist, but he didn't work with me directly. He was a Christian. Malayali Christian. Or Mallu, as we call them in India.

In retrospect, I think Biju was the braver man. He took risks. I mean, he could afford to take risks. He left his comfort zone to experience life and the world, as he put it. All this settling down stuff, wife, children, house, big car and a paunch, not for me, boss, not for me, he often said. The same sentence every time. He was, of course, thoughtful enough to suggest that such a life was perfectly suited to my temperament. At other times, he cursed the place where we were: 'cloistered like indentured labour, in a prison, boss, this is a cage disguised as a place of comfort, boss, where we tell ourselves we are happy'. His words, not mine. And he was comprehensively wrong.

His cavalier attitude towards life, towards the world, really ... was something I hadn't witnessed before. His disdain for authority, in particular for the non-clinical staff, especially for Sir Farhad's Chief Secretary, was, how do I say ... rather out of place, and sometimes, completely out of order. I'll tell you about it, of course I will.

One thing at a time, my dear, one thing at a time. There's so much to say, so much to show from under the cobwebs of time and age. I'm an old man now, so please allow me to take my time, Sara. I promise not to take forever, of course. I don't have forever.

You may remember Biju; he came home a few times when you were little. He was very nice to you. It doesn't matter if you don't remember. You don't have to remember him; you were very small. I'll tell you more about him later. He was funny; strange and funny.

~

Most patients who came to Emergency complained of stomach aches, headaches and body aches. We gave them Buscopan injections because almost everyone asked for Buscopan injections. Sometimes via IV too. Administering the medicines wasn't the problem. Treating female patients, while their male companions, husbands and fathers mostly, stood over your head, was. I must admit my hands once trembled while taking an old woman's temperature. Her husband glared at me the whole time. What did he think I was going to do, seduce her via the glass vial? Thank god, checking for fever was the extent of physical examination we were supposed to carry out on women. Unless, of course, it was a life-or-death situation. I wanted to ask my bosses how one was to save a life if one's own life was under threat from an extra-vigilant husband or brother.

Very few patients stayed overnight, even when we said it was best to spend the night. They simply refused and left. I told myself it would get better with time, as I gained more authority.

Later, Biju told me it wasn't unusual for some patients, especially older ones, to ask for a second opinion if a female doctor had seen them. Even if the second examiner was a new recruit, a junior, like me.

Nevertheless, some female patients refused to be seen by a man, especially if it was a foreign man. They preferred to wait for the next available female doctor. It was all too confusing at first, even though I knew some of the reasons. To put it simply, it wasn't easy to strike a balance between 'cultural sensitivity' (as it said on the laminated manual for newcomers) and your responsibilities as a professional. So, the quickest lesson I learnt over there was, 'Do as told. Don't think too much.' Luckily, we only had minor cases at first. The seriously injured were flown to the super-speciality institute in the port city nearby. We had a helipad on the roof, with an old, made-in-the

USSR chopper parked and chained to metal girders. Biju and I went up to see it one day. It was boring.

—

In six months or so, I was looking at minor accident cases, patching up injured legs and arms. Also treating domestic workers who had almost always had a fall. Oh, the sutures were so fine and easy to work with, all imported from Germany. I even performed little surgeries sometimes, and I have to say it was excellent practice. I wasn't qualified to do so, but the Chief Secretary had let it be known that it was alright as long I did it under supervision. I didn't tell him or anyone else that the only senior with us either looked the other way, or was on yet another coffee or smoke or toilet break. He didn't work much and we didn't complain.

5

You see, Sara, it had to happen ... I couldn't have prevented it, could I? It could have been anyone, and it was me. It had to happen to someone, and it was me. Think about it. Of all the men in the world, of all the doctors in the world, of all the fathers in the whole world, I happened to be the one present in that place at that time. Someone or the other had to do it. It just so happens that that someone was your dad. That's how I look at it now, anyway. I didn't choose to be there, did I? It was all predestined, don't you think?

You know, I was quite young when I left home for England. Who was to know I wouldn't last even two full years here then? Anyhow, I was such a star in the neighbourhood when people heard I was going abroad. Abbu walked in the streets as if he'd vanquished all his troubles and foes and become the badshah of the locality. After all, I was the first person in the entire clan to be going to a Western country. Some distant relatives had spent years working in the Gulf, but no one had seen a proper foreign city. And to top it all, I was headed to London. Vilayat, as my mother said to anyone who listened or didn't listen. Ammi gave alms so many times a day to stave off the evil eye that Shabi, my sister, joked we'd soon be begging for food ourselves. For weeks, aunts, uncles, neighbours and family friends came to congratulate my parents. Everyone brought sweets that practically oozed type 2 diabetes.

Shabi said I shouldn't feel too flattered, as nearly everyone who came to visit was fishing for a match for their daughter or niece. 'You think these women who have never set foot in our house would be landing wet kisses on you if they didn't have marriageable daughters or sisters?'

I said it was flattering nonetheless.

'Let's see how flattered you feel when you meet one of the girls.'

'Please spare me,' I said.

'No, no, you must. I know a few of these worthies, brother. One is so bright, so bright ... that she spent five years doing her Matric just to make her mark. Another is properly stunning, until she opens her mouth, that is. Breathtakingly beautiful, ha-ha. I know her a little better than I know the others. Shall I arrange a date, marriage-material bro?' Shabi could be ruthless like that, but she was also very protective of me. It was through her that I met Atiya. You know that, right? They went to the same teacher-training programme in Meerut, Atiya's town, and became friends on the first day.

So, you see, I left home for England, but look where I landed. Fate moves in small circles over our heads, just to toss us around, don't you think? It was destined to be me. And it's not as if it was my main occupation. Oh no, far,

far from it. I had a perfectly ordinary job on most days. How did it all begin? When was the first time? What did it feel like? I'll come to it all, I promise.

I've been meaning to say this for so many years, Sara. I've thought and rethought the words so many times that the perfect words may have already escaped me, or they never arrived. And maybe they never will. That's why I will just say it as it is. As it was.

—

I was there, Sara, I was there. In the thick of it, in the middle of it all. I'd do it and then get back to routine work. Even though what was routine and what wasn't became mixed up sometimes. I'd do it, and then have tea and biscuits with my colleagues. Of course, I couldn't tell them all at first. What could I tell them? That I was the chosen one, selected to do it, and that I was paid extra? Please don't ask how much. It's embarrassing.

Once or twice a year, or every couple of years, it felt as if a small battle was going on somewhere nearby and I was on call to have the wounds fixed and dressed. I was there: closing the wounds, healing the wounds, then seeing those faces at night. There were, of course, the dreams. I'd wake up startled, having seen one of the faces in the dark. Sometimes they shook hands with me. Even in my dreams, I'd remind myself to shake hands properly. Not the limp, passive shake that can be construed as a sign of weakness, disinterest, or a lack of manners. I would've just shaken a hand and I'd be wide awake, confused, sometimes holding my other hand. In all honesty, it didn't happen every night. Some nights I slept normally.

~

One day, they brought two people whose time was up. Let me work out what year it was. Sometimes certainty deserts me, but this I remember clearly. It was my third year over there and I think a few months after Sir Farhad decided to have such cases shifted from Corrections to the hospital. You weren't born yet.

The two men had been convicted of selling stolen electronic goods. I didn't always know the deeds of those we attended to. This was also one of the few occasions when those I had to supervise were natives. I brought it upon myself, I admit, I'll tell you about it.

Anyhow, earlier that day, I was walking back from the toilets when I saw the Chief Secretary. He rarely came to see me for anything else, so I went along quietly. He always smelled of green cardamom. We first went to Sir Farhad's office on the first floor, which was unusual, much as I liked being in his enormous office. As I entered, Sir Farhad stood up and said, 'It should've been quick, that was the idea, wasn't it, but the Great Judge wants to preside over the proceedings. It appears to me that he wants to observe and make sure. I don't understand why. I am here. Am I not? Who am I?'

'You're the boss,' the Chief Secretary said, but Farhad didn't even look at him.

'I believe he wants to be acknowledged as the

preeminent jurist of our time, and it appears to me that that's the reason why he hasn't shown any leniency. The father and son are our people, somewhat known in their neighbourhood. I may have known of them too. There were suggestions from some quarters that perhaps the honourable judge might be kinder to the father, or at least be open to the idea of commuting the punishment. Although, according to me, if anyone deserves mercy, it has to be the son. He has a full life ahead—fruitful employment, marriage, babies, and service to the community. However, the Great Judge has made it a point that there'll be no amendments to the decree just because they are our own, as it's against the law. And he is the law ... So there we go. I am the administrator, and he knows I can't go against his decision without a major breach of protocol. Clever old fox.'

At first, I thought the Director was talking to me, but he was actually speaking into the space-age apparatus on his desk. Or maybe he was dictating to a machine linked to it. He spoke in English. Sir Farhad was a mysterious man and remained so until the very end. He smoked now, and walked up and down the length of his desk. He lit another cigarillo, took only two or three drags, and stubbed it out. This was the first time that I'd heard he was 'The Administrator'. Not only did he run the hospital where I worked, but he also ran the town where I lived! Why hadn't I been told? I felt silly. This was also the first time I'd seen someone smoke a cigarillo.

I should ask Sara if she smokes, shouldn't I? Perhaps not. That's not what good fathers do, put their children in a spot. It's best not to ask and not know. Don't ask, don't tell, as they say.

'Thank god, you're here, Dr K, let's go,' Sir Farhad said and left the room. He'd started calling me Dr K a couple of months after I joined; it was probably the one thing I didn't like about him.

We followed him to his personal lift and went up to the top floor where the refitted hall was. The lift was meant for his exclusive use. It smelled of cologne. I tried to look for vents from where the scent came, but there were only the AC vents in the ceiling. Maybe the cold air meant for this lift was premixed with scent, because I didn't detect any scent in the other lifts, apart from the smell of cleaning liquids or sometimes Biju's cigarette and post-drinking breath. It hadn't occurred to me before, but I was curious now about how they managed to air-condition the elevators as they moved up and down.

Just a procedure, just a small procedure, I kept telling myself, as we went up. I remember feeling the same sort of nervousnes I used to feel in high school when it was time for the science viva voce. I would know everything, but to appear in front of the teachers and answer their questions felt like walking through a tree. My mouth would feel so dry that I worried whether I'd be able to open it at all. The viva took place in the hall on the ground floor of our college. The cursed door was right in the centre. There was nowhere to hide after I entered. I would walk the ten or twelve steps to the desk on which my notebook was open, a record of all the science experiments for the term. One of the teachers would always fiddle with it. They'd smile but, uff, by the time I somehow managed to walk up to them, I'd be dizzy. I rarely did well in the viva.

—

The father and son were already strapped, anaesthetised, all ready. They wore white robes that stretched to their feet. They could have been two men waiting for their favourite hairdresser or masseuse. I tried to imagine the words they might have exchanged in the morning. Who gave whom support? Who was the stronger of the two? What words did they say to the family before leaving? Did they have breakfast before setting off? What did the son say to his mother? What did the father say to his wife? And what did the mother say to the son? Did anyone grieve, chant a dirge?

Quite suddenly, I thought of Abbu, who'd started taking driving lessons back home in Saharanpur. I shrugged him off and started for the duo. Bright light lit up every little corner and crevice in the hall, as if it were one of those day-and-night cricket matches that had started lately. It was too bright. I'd have to change the lights near my patients, I decided. The staff here still hadn't understood we needed beams, not floodlights. It had already been a few months since the arrangement was formalised. Fools. And for god's sake, why was it freezing? In all fairness, not too many locals were obsessed with ice-cold air-conditioning; it was often the overseas staff who, probably scared by visions of being baked into a chapatti, turned the knobs to max whenever they got a chance. I'd become much better at handling the chill after I discovered how cosy I felt in my light leather jacket.

Didn't someone say the mind is its own place, it can make a heaven of hell, a hell of heaven, or something like that? I remember trying hard but I just couldn't keep my father from my mind. He had this uncanny ability to get into my head at the strangest of times. Thank god, he hadn't become a speaking ghost. Ammi hadn't been too happy with his decision to learn to drive. 'Son, even with the driver, he insists on crawling. It takes us more than an hour to get vegetables from Khanna Market next door. If he starts driving, I'll have to put a gas stove in the car itself,' she'd said to me. Luckily, things hadn't yet come to a head; many months into his lessons at Sharma's Excellent Driving Institute, Abbu was still struggling with the ABC of it.

Anyhow, I gave up trying to expel him, and walked on. The Great Judge and a few other officials sat on curved sofas by the wall. Two large men stood on either side of the man who wanted to be known as a great jurist of his time. This was not the first time I'd be watched while supervising the performance, but it was the first time I had a VIP in the audience. There was a tea set on the table by the sofa. It was the colour of silver, or made of silver. I know that sounds like a cliché, but trust me, Sara, it's true. I saw it. And I wanted a cuppa too, but didn't ask. The judge's robe had wide gold-and-black piping on the margins. He wore a sleek dark headdress, and his beard glimmered in the white light. I thought he exuded authority and grace. An elegant rosary was wrapped around his wrist, I saw it. Near the papers sat a PDA. I'd just seen these on cable TV, for god's sake, and he or one of his assistants already had one.

I set to work after tuning down the lights, switching off anything that shone directly into my eyes. At first, however, I was once again stalled by indecision, as the assistants waited for my directions: do we go for the father or the son first? Maybe I was more anxious than usual because of the judge and the others. I have to say the Director never worried me. He was never intrusive and rarely talked during the procedures, if at all. After all, I was doing his work. He would just watch. Later, he didn't even come to many of the ops. And I must say, Sara, I'd be a bit disappointed. He was always nice to me, right until the end.

Anyhow, I decided to work on the father first, just in case there was a miraculous, last-minute change of heart in the judge. Or a phone call from a higher authority. Like in films. But you see, my dear, films are films and real life is real life. So, I went into auto-mode and had the Great Judge's orders executed. Or the orders of the hospital director who was also the town's ruler.

I had no choice, Sara, which is the simple and absolute truth. It was my job. Maybe because it was the first procedure in front of the watchful eyes of an important man, or perhaps because Abbu kept knocking inside my head and I really wanted him to back off, I asked one of the paras to pick up the excised things and briefly display them for the judge and the director. I don't know why I did that. I still don't. I have scratched my head, my memory, my heart, for years and I still don't. In all probability, I never will.

Madness. Sadness.

I do, however, clearly remember that I felt cold immediately afterwards. I'd probably broken into a sweat, or the chill of the ACs had seeped through my clothes. I saw my knuckles had turned white. I didn't speak to anyone.

—

If I'd told Sara all this when she was younger, she might not have taken it well. Asked questions I'd have no answers to. Now, it's a different matter altogether. We are both adults.

I'll tell Sara that, sometimes, when I had the opportunity, I would slip a few diazepam strips into the patient's or an attendant's pocket or hand. It was always strange and most saddening to touch the other hand. Have I already told you this bit? I wasn't allowed to give them analgesics at the time. (Of course, I knew exactly what happened after the anaesthetic wore off.) How could I be so uncaring and cruel towards my patients? I knew that if I was caught I could always explain it to Farhad. Didn't he himself say that it should all be modernised, made more humane, in line with contemporary procedures? Didn't he smile? For god's sake, sir jee, you built us a new theatre, I'd say to him, what use is it if we don't also change our approach, our entire ethic! If nothing worked, I'd explain the epidemiological background of phantom pain to him; he was a man who liked to know new things. If absolutely nothing worked, I'd argue that diazepam is not an analgesic.

Anyhow, it was sad and embarrassing that, in front of the Great Judge and his large minions, I lost my nerve. Performance anxiety, I called it later. I didn't even try to pass on the tabs, neither to the father, nor to the son. They stayed in my coat pocket for some time, as daily reminders of my guilt and torment until, many washes later, they crumbled into dirt along with the packaging.

I'll tell her this too. I have to. I'm sure I can tell her anything now, even if it's not very flattering. I am her father, for god's sake, she'll have to listen. If she doesn't, who will?

I didn't stay to see the father and son off. They had many relatives waiting downstairs.

6

THE FATHER AND SON WERE not my first case, and yet I remember the day I saw them as the day it all started. Looking back, reassessing, I have come to conclude that whatever happened prior to that day in the July of that year was all a prelude.

Out there at Corrections or down in the busy Emergency, we'd get it done and forget about it. *Sort of* forget is what I mean, of course. It happened occasionally, and I quickly consigned it to the past, to the done-and-dusted bin. I'd be relieved that we didn't have to carry out another procedure for months, years. And clearly it was best to carry on with normal duties and life, I told myself. Starting with tending to botched procedures at Corrections, healing messed-up hands, and then having to do it ourselves, amid other cases, so that we didn't have to mend messed-up hands, felt like a temporary but necessary thing. Part of my duty. For the first year or so after that first call from Corrections, there was no doubt in my mind that we fixed other people's mess. And it was true—that's what we did at the Emergency, fix things, isn't it? I was and I remain a helpful person, I think.

You see, Sara, I've spent all these years trying to make

sense of it. We'd do it—it was the only sensible, *professional*, thing to do—and we'd then try to forget about it. I thought about it often but I rarely lost my equilibrium.

I try to make sense of it, even though I may not have the when, how, who down very precisely. The order of things isn't important. What it means is, don't you think? Still, I'll try to tell you everything precisely and in the correct order, as much as is possible for me now. It's a peculiar thing, memory. It was so long ago and yet everything writhes in my head somewhere. People lie when they say, oh, my memory fails me, I just can't remember ... It's always there, isn't it? I mean, it may not pop up when you need to prove a point but it's always there, slithering around inside your head. The denial of self-deception is the ruse of self-deception, I've felt sometimes. Deep down, you know the truth. In your heart of hearts, you know when you lie or speak the truth. The rest is noise, as rich people and their therapists remind each other.

I'm curious to know if Sara might say, 'Did they compel you to do it, Dad?' I'll have to give her an honest answer.

No, I've got to be honest, my dear, no one forced me. I'm a professional. I got into it incrementally but intentionally. Along with a couple of others in the department, of course. Only very occasionally do I think there might have been a plan to it all along. That maybe Sir Farhad always knew he wanted someone in his own hospital to take charge of it. That they then set in motion an elaborate chain of events, a complex and complicated process, during which I chose to volunteer in a good cause. That, while I felt it was my duty to be of help, Sir Farhad, or whoever it was, had had their eyes on a fresh immigrant all along. There was perhaps a note in a file somewhere in the Chief Secretary's cabinets:

Indian Man. Grateful, respects authority, well read, family man. Model immigrant, perfect candidate.

But you see, when I think of it that way, it begins to smell of a detailed conspiracy, and I'm not so credulous as to embrace the first conspiracy theory that explains everything about the universe and my place in it. Besides, Sir Farhad was a genuinely good man. Trust me. A legitimate leader who wanted to bring about change, improve an age-old practice in his province. And he liked me. Yes, in a general sense, the world and our lives in it are all part of an elaborate conspiracy. What is destiny but an intricate scheme, a saazish, a plan?

~

Anyhow, I want to tell her everything I remember without guiding her judgement. I want to tell her so that she can judge for herself. I want to tell her so she can form an independent opinion—a character sketch, if I may—of her father.

Why else have I waited for so long?

And if at the end of it Sara decides that I have erred, or worse, committed a sin, I'll be happy to bow my head before my daughter. There's no shame in that.

7

I CAN'T BE A HUNDRED per cent certain, but I believe she'll understand everything. I'm sure of it. She's my only child, after all.

I want to tell her there came a time when I sensed I had crossed over into some other world and it was lonely there; I had no one to look at but myself. [When Sara comes, I'll at last have someone else to look at and to talk to in the darkness.] Yes, it was something like that. You cross a barrier between the usual, ordinary world, and the unusual, extraordinary one. Strangely, by this time, I was no longer tense during the surgeries. Just quiet. I had a good, kind hand, they said. I wondered how they felt, those who saw my marker-bearing hand on theirs. I still think about that sometimes, quite often as a matter of fact. Our elders used to say that quiet contemplation is the most meaningful way to live life's later years.

~

Of course, at first, I had no idea I'd become part of a special group of people who, you know, do the kind of thing ordinary people don't. People like me are interviewed in the press about our work, aren't we? We are the subject of weekend articles. Special Features. You know, one of those things they print on shiny paper. The photographs are, of course, black-and-white, to go with the subject matter, I suppose. They think people like me must live in perennial darkness, outside the frame, outside the light of normal days and nights. I'm not entirely sure of that, though.

When did you decide on this line of work?

How does it feel?

Do you have a family?

Do you have dreams?

No one decides to do it, you fools. At least I didn't. It's not as if I was asked in school what I wanted to be when I grew up, and I said 'punishment-surgeon'. Somehow or the other, you drift into it. What else?

No, I don't have a family. I landed from Krypton wearing a white coat!

How do you sleep at night, how do you hold, feed and bathe your little girl? How do you show love to your daughter? That's what they should be asking. Imbeciles.

Then, and this has taken me decades to understand, the abnormal too becomes the normal. I read somewhere that if man can get used to murder, he can get used to anything. You remain somewhat different to the outside normal, but within, you are ordinarised (if that's a word), normalised (that *is* a word), and that's when it hits you. To be honest, I don't remember the precise moment it happened to me, but now I am the person who has seen it all, to whom all of it has happened, and I have finally surfaced to tell you about it. Mine is also a vastly different case, don't you think?

Well, because my substantive job was normal, like everyone else's. It's not as if I did the other thing every day, is it? But yes, I admit, it's what I did occasionally, on the side, that's stayed with me. Why wouldn't it?

Although, from a strictly professional point of view, why would it?

Over ten years or so, let's say … I must've seen maybe fifteen, eighteen, or twenty such cases—alright, maybe a few more if I stretch it. The arithmetic isn't the issue. It's quite simple if I put my mind to it. Let's see. We started the procedures formally in my third year at the hospital, or just before you were born. I remember because I was expecting a promotion at the time, and they did make me Assistant Medical Superintendent to Abdel Hamad's MS. Then, I count until the year Atiya left us, and then a few more years until Biju went back to India.

Every time I think about those days, I'm confused about the moments when maybe I could've made a choice. But I also know it's all retrospective. The choice appears because there are more than two decades between me then and me now. Because, now, post facto, I'm removed from it all, am I not? What puzzles me still, though, is that I don't remember feeling numb. It was so … how do I describe the feeling … both ordinary and extraordinary?

The past remains with you, no matter what. It's silly when people say, oh, the past catches up with you, it haunts you, and so on. I've always carried it with me. It's here, there, everywhere … under my very skin. Every day that I live carries images, moments and words from that time. Every time I look down at this city of riches and splendour, I remember that other city and the mile within it that contained my life. Occasionally, the long distance between the two gives me some comfort.

I want to tell Sara that I don't like hospitals any more. I'll ask her to pray that I never have to visit one again. When it's time for me to join Atiya, I'd like to leave from here, my own home. I can't be sure if Sara will be here then. I'd, of course, like to see her one last time. Please do come, Sara.

And I have full faith that she'll come. If not this year, then the next ... But I'm not sure I can trust life. I mean, no one can. Sara is the one mirror, the one counterbalance, to my history. She's the future I dreamt of ages ago. She's the promise that emerged from the void. This, too, is the reason I've kept her removed from myself. Now I don't want to leave without giving her my life's account.

All I want in life now is for her to listen to me.

PART II

8

I'll tell her, when I first came to England thirty-four years ago, I was quite young. Twenty-seven to be precise; not even two years older than she is now. She knows very little about my arrival. Or about my departure, for that matter.

I was excited, keen to work hard, make a life, travel, and I did work very, very hard in those two years. But I felt lost. I felt invisible. As if I was no one.

And it was aggravating when people sometimes murmured, oh, wish these new people had a little more self-awareness. That's all we got, folks, I wanted to scream back.

All I wanted to do was put my head down, work, be nice, save money and make a home of my own, but I just didn't feel I fitted in. Or so I thought then. You see, a fresh immigrant's mind is in a state of perennial confusion, pulled as it is in various directions. You want to look ahead, but you find yourself looking over your shoulder. You don't want to remember you're a migrant all the time, but everything around you reminds you of it. Soon, you become suspicious of yourself. Do you understand? At the bus stop, you make a complete fool of yourself by rushing in ahead of an old woman, or by waiting until everyone has slipped in and finding there's no room left.

One day, in my first year here, I was waiting at a bus stop near a paan, sweets and video shop that overlooked a square in Queensbury, a sterile, dead sort of suburb on the Jubilee Line. Really, it felt so lifeless that I could die of boredom or sadness there. It was the middle of the day, in the middle of the damp and depressing winter. I was visiting a college senior who I'd been told was doing very well in less than three years of arriving in England. Reports travelled from home (Shabi called it the gossipgram) that he already had a four-wheel drive and a house of his own in a posh area of London. Posh, my foot. I mean, it was green and clean and had all the prettiness of a foreign suburb, but I didn't see a soul on the broad and leafy streets. Akhil had been the college topper two years before me, but nothing he said was news. Locum-Locum, Nights-Nights ... is all he said. Apart from tips on how to save pounds, that is: buy all your clothes, routine meds, painkillers and toiletries when you go home once a year. I wanted to ask if this applied to soap and underwear too. Anyhow, when the bus came, I went for the door in the middle, thinking why add to the crowd at the front. But the moment I tried to put my foot in, an old man said, 'In this country, we wait for our turn, young man, and you've got the wrong door.' I still remember the hot flush that swept across my face.

I'm not suggesting I wasn't treated well. That would be dishonest. Maybe I had a flawed expectation of what it meant to fit in. Maybe I was trying too hard to act normal. Sometimes I think that, despite my best efforts, I couldn't convince England that, maybe, I didn't want to be treated in any way, either specially or un-specially. Is it possible that I might have wanted to be seen as an equal? I know that back then I thought I should just be myself and not try too hard to blend in. Although, despite all that, I swear I did try, as much as I could in my own lazy way. I went to a few parties too, but it was always the same thing.

I even went to a Christmas dinner once. Some colleagues at St James's had booked a rustic restaurant by the river. Its ceiling was uncovered. You could see shafts of old black and pale wood propped by bent pillars. For a moment, I expected to see bird nests in some corner or crevice. No, Sara, I'm not joking. The dinner was fine, I ate what I wanted to. In all fairness, the office manager had asked me about pork, and I'd said, no, I don't eat pork. It's not because of religion etcetera, it's just that I'm not used to it, I mean, I'm conditioned not to eat it. Later, I asked myself why I said that to him, the religion bit. This was a time when your dad didn't know pork and ham were the same meat.

Anyhow, at the dinner, everyone was in a cheerful mood and I thought to myself that Christmas is such a joyous occasion for these people. It truly was. I now knew exactly why people said Merry Christmas, Merry Christmas all the time, even to strangers.

After about three hours in that hard rustic chair, the boss said to me, 'You are coming to the party at mine after, aren't you? Now, now, Kaiser, come on, don't you tell me you aren't!' I didn't know what to say. No one had asked me, but maybe he thought he had, so I said yes, yes, of course, I'm coming, sir. This was my first year in England. At the party (I loved his house and the long garden that even had a swing at the back), I tried to mix, somewhat self-consciously, I must admit. I pretended to be busy looking at their bookshelf, studying the spines one by one, because after the customary race-check hellos and handshakes, I was, well, I was alone. I wish people didn't make too conscious an effort to make you feel comfortable, because when they leave to find the next person who needs to be made comfortable, you feel as if you're naked. I'm sure at some level it must grate on both parties.

At some point that night, the boss's wife, all pink and red-eyed, came towards me. She was taller than me, so I subtly raised my heels on to the base of the fireplace I'd been admiring. I wondered how they managed to light it, given that everything was behind a glass casing. She was drinking something pink-ish. I'd never ever seen anyone drink a pink drink before, apart from Rooh Afza back home, but that's more ruby-red than pink.

'I am terribly sorry, erm, mister …? I've completely forgotten your name, Tristan did mention it, I'm sure … It must be all the booze I've had since lunch.'

I didn't know what to say.

'Had you for a mo there, eh!' She tugged at my arm. 'Don't worry, only a few tiny tipples, I assure you, daahling.'

I smiled a little.

'So, are you going to tell me your name, or shall it remain a mystery? I'm Deborah, by the way.'

She could've simply asked her husband again, I thought.

'Oh, he's out there in the garden, cigar time for the gents, you see. I don't allow that in the house. Na-na. The smell tends to live on in the sofas and the cushions and the curtains forever.'

'I am Kaiser, Dr Kaiser Shah, and you must be Mrs Tristan?'

'Nice to meet you, Keyser. Yes, guilty as charged. Please call me Deborah.'

'Nice to meet you too, Madam.' I had to look down immediately, because not one but two buttons on her shirt had come undone, and she didn't seem to mind it.

I was also puzzled why she felt 'guilty as charged' when I called her Mrs Tristan. It was all a bit strange. Before she moved on to the other guests, she asked me where I came from, if I was comfortable, and if there was anything I needed. I have to say it was nice of her, even if I'd have preferred it if she hadn't called me something like 'geyser'. She must have spent four or five minutes with me, but it felt like a lot longer.

Soon, I turned back to the bookshelves.

—

Integration, I've come to understand, Sara, is basically a part of the migrant–immigrant–refugee's job description. They should just say it at the top. Integrate, assimilate, or else.

Or else what? Annihilate, immolate, evaporate, disintegrate?

As if living a castaway's life wasn't lonely enough. First, you arrive a little lost, a little tired, but full of dreams and promise, wary but also excited, a little bit scared but also hopeful, your visa an entry card to a new life and new dreams, and then you're expected to make an effort to fit in, to be like the natives, behave like they do. Or, to be multi-culti, by which they mean to say, come to our party, be open-minded, and it might be interesting if you put on your ethnic gear, preferably multicoloured, preferably topped with peacock or parrot or minaret headgear ... But, but, I've always worn suits, sirs and madams, ever since I graduated and took the oath. Guess why? Because your good old gora sahibs ruled us for ages, told us it was the civilised thing to do, gentlemanly stuff and what not! Now, I come to your land wearing my finest suit, my only pinstripe, but you'd like it more if I went back to my kurta-pyjama and jewelled sandals and bling headgear. Well, guess what, many of us don't do bling. I certainly don't. And, by the way, the turban is your Sikh friend, not me. The garland is your Hindu holy man, or charlatan, or that Beatle person, what was his name—George Harrison—not me. Yes, fine, alright, the skullcap would be me, but only on Fridays and Eid. You got that bit right.

I didn't say any of that at the time, Sara. I wish I had. Bling is a word I learnt later in life. As I said, I was confused, dazzled and depressed by turn, or all those things at the same time. I can laugh it off now, of course.

I think she'll enjoy this part. I'm sure she will.

9

IF SHE ASKS, AND ASK she will, I'll tell her no, I do not feel shame. It's something more than, beyond, shame. I can't tell you how I feel. You know how I feel. Sometimes I wonder if there are other people like me out there, having done or doing the kind of thing I've done. I've *had* to do. At other times, I think, what if I am the only one, *one of a kind*, you know. Either possibility instils in me the same feeling, and I don't know which is worse. I really don't.

She'll probably look at me in that slanting way, with one eyebrow arched, I know, but it's time I told her the full story. Uff, to have to second-guess someone you haven't met for years and long to meet every day is like a curse you can't do without.

When I try to imagine the others, Sara, I can't really see them, only myself. But I think about them all the same. Quite a few people, you know, a biradari, a fraternity of men who, you know, do the exact same thing: cut, chop and fix. What if, I've asked myself several times, there are people like me in that other country, in the next town, or in your country, for that matter? What if it's simple demand and supply? You know, a small industry consisting of people like me. What if there's a recruitment agency somewhere that scouts for people like your father and places them in organisations suited to their skill-set. A perfect fit, you see. Come on, of course it's possible.

It is, after all, a medical professional who examines, let's say, a death-row convict before they drape the noose around him. Is it not?

It is a doctor who certifies death after execution by the needle.

It is a GP who conducts a check-up before someone's beheaded, or hung by a crane, or after someone's asked to sit in the electric chair.

It's a doctor, for god's sake, who waits for a few seconds for the body to cool down from the jolts to check if that heart's still beating.

They are all my co-workers, are they not? My fraternity, as I said.

~

When she has rested for a day or two, I'll give her the full, uncensored account. Tell her about what it was really like, about my friendship with Sir Farhad, and with Biju, of course. I suspect she'd like to hear all about Biju and me, and I'll tell her, I have to, although it's not going to be easy. God only knows what her relatives from Atiya's side have told her. The last time she visited, she was a teenager. I don't complain much. She's been extremely busy. These are, after all, the formative years of her career and she's doing very well, Mashallah. First, the hard years at business school, then internship and probation, she said once. It takes longer in America, I know.

I must make sure, I will make sure, that I don't tell her about the bad dream I sometimes have of her having been dead all this time, since the time she went to America. And that she's grown up to be a brilliant young woman only in my mind. It will make her sad.

She doesn't call much either, which is fine, I suppose. She must work hard during the week and weekends must be full of chores and friends. I'm sure she's popular; she's an attractive girl, after all. And then there's the time difference.

I'm not too sure if I should ask about her boyfriend. Does she even have one, given how busy she is? Is it the done thing to ask your grown-up daughter about her love life? Catherine disappears just when I need her the most. I could use a bit of advice now.

—

Tell me something, Sara, I'll say to her, just to break the ice further. Have I told you about Catherine?

Yes, a little bit, but not really. Who is she, Dad?

Someone's curious! Well now, I have known Catherine for five or six years. Goodness, it feels like yesterday and it's already been such a long time. We met at The Mongoose. She was sitting alone by the bar. I was sitting alone in the leather chair by the fireplace. The idiots threw it out a few years ago and I stopped going there. I mean, I don't go as often as I used to. I hardly go out now.

Anyhow, we were perhaps the only two people in the pub without any company. It was a nice, warm evening a couple of weeks before Christmas. Green and red trinkets hung bright atop the bar. People were unusually nice or just happily drunk. Festive cheer, we call it here.

I know, Dad.

Of course you know. Anyhow, I spotted Terry, the landlord, talking to a woman. He looked in my direction a couple of times. She had her back towards me. I thought, for a woman, she sat rather inelegantly on the stool. Then I quickly corrected myself. Would I say the same thing if it were a man?

As I tried to work my way through the Times Crossword, a shadow hovered over the squares. I knew it was the woman from the bar. Honestly, I don't know why she came over. I might have been better looking in those days, but a white woman, or any woman, who drank alone, trying to strike up a conversation with me? That was a first. Or maybe it was precisely because she was someone who drank alone in pubs.

Oh, come on, Dad, you are still dashing, Sara might say. Will she? Yes, she might.

You're beginning to embarrass me, I'll say then.

Anyhow, do you mind if I sit here, Catherine said, and she sat down without waiting for an answer. I couldn't help breaking into a big smile, I remember. I hadn't been this close to a woman since your mother, you know...

I know, I know, Dad, I'm sure you'll spare me the details.

Oh, nothing of the sort, my dear, nothing of the sort. You don't have to worry. Catherine and I are, well, we call ourselves occasional friends. Like the occasional half, get it?

I cook for her sometimes. She comes home after a drink or two at that same pub. We eat and talk, but not too much. Then she goes home. Then I don't see her for some time. Then we meet again, exactly like the last time. It's not like I'm in love with her, please. But would you like to meet her?

Would you like me to meet her?

I don't mind. She's brilliant.

You're such a Brit, Dad.

No, I'm not.

Yes, you are.

Have I told you Catherine is very slightly squint-eyed, but we've never talked about it? I have noticed. She's noticed that I have. It's rude to ask, isn't it? People call her Cath, but I'm not able to. I've tried, but it's just not her. For me, she's Catherine and that's that, I told myself.

On second thoughts, I'm not sure if I should talk too much about Catherine. It might make Sara uncomfortable, even though it isn't really something that might be called a romantic liaison. Catherine and I don't even have a relationship. She's kind and nice to me, and I like her.

~

Many years ago, not long after you left, Sara, I used to find my hands touching each other at night, scratching at the knuckles and the wrist. I'd wake up, or maybe I'd be half-awake through it all, and find there was no itching. I'd feel a distinct sensation on the back of my hands, but that's it. No scratch marks. Nothing. Sometimes I'd pull my left hand with my right and vice versa. Just to reassure myself that they're normal. Just to check whether I am normal.

I'd stroke my fingers and wrist over and over, until I'd feel sleepy again or it was time to get out of bed. But that was many years ago. It, the real or imagined itch, stopped.

Do you have to talk about it today, Dad? I'm here for a few weeks, she might say.

Oh, yes, yes, now that you say it, I don't have to do it now. How silly of me. It's just that I have waited so long, and seeing you here, at last, I didn't consider whether I should or shouldn't talk about it now. I am sorry, I didn't pause to think. I just started, didn't I? I feel I probably don't really have a choice in the matter, but yes, we can certainly do it tomorrow, or the day after, when you're fully de-jet-lagged, eh. And you can surely stay for a few more days if I'm not done, can't you?

How was the flight, by the way? Comfortable, I hope? Virgin is a decent airline, although I find that Branson chap a bit too showy for my taste. Tedious, is it not, seeing the man peddle his stuff all the time? In any case, I've always been a bit suspicious of men with half-beards.

Oh, I forgot to ask, Sara, would you like to go to the London Eye tomorrow?

Come on, Dad, I'm not fourteen any more. You remember the summer I was visiting and Mummy's relatives landed up for the holidays? I must have, like, gone to the Eye at least three times. Thank god, no one stayed with you then! By the end of it, I wanted to jump into the river, so thanks but no thanks.

Alright, alright. I just wanted to check...

So, I was saying ... I don't know what to call it, the thing I feel in my heart. It's always there, all the time, like a dark and corrosive drip. Let me put it this way. Every time I look into the distance, or at a wall, or when I'm still, my mind goes back to those days. I feel powerless against it, and then I decide not to fight it. I go over everything again and again, and only then does it lighten a bit. My chest.

~

Yes, I did speak with Uncle Biju about it, just so you know. It was impossible to keep it under wraps after the Department of Corrections started sending us cases from time to time. And with a designated theatre on the top floor, however restricted it was, Biju was bound to find out. So, I felt it was best he heard it from me. He was a dear friend, after all, and we were perfectly normal back then. Obviously, I didn't tell him everything. Funny man, guess what he said? Give me a monthly cut from your double-decker salary, K, and I'll put in a word for you at the Church when I go home next. They can have an exclusive prayer for you every Sunday, but that might cost a little more. Ours is the second oldest diocese in Kerala, and my father is a friend of the father, ha.

Biju could be like that even on the most sombre occasion. Then again, I think, better that than a brooding friend in the corner. You have your own cares and worries, your own battles to fight, and if you also have to massage a weak-hearted mate now and then, who will you talk to? If only he hadn't messed up, Sara, if only ... As the great Momin said, 'What wouldn't have been possible in the world if only you had been mine?' That reminds me, did you know that, apart from being one of the greatest poets of the Urdu language, Momin was a trained medical practitioner from a family of well-known hakeems? I didn't know either until recently. Anyhow, enough about Biju, I don't want him to butt in on this too. Our time together.

As you wish, Dad.

I have a strong feeling Sara might want to know more about Biju. Uncle Biju! But I'm also absolutely sure she'll understand if I take my time.

10

Have I ever told you about Aapa?

She was Ammi's aunt, your great grand-aunt, that is. Kind old woman who'd never married and lived in the ancestral maternal home near Rampur. I probably never told you, or maybe I have, that my mother's family, like Atiya's, had been minor nobles at some point in the past. They retained their name, airs and the wobbly, dusty haveli near Rampur but, clearly, none of their wealth. Abbu sometimes joked that they had, in fact, been actors who played noblemen and women in dramas staged for the real nawabs of Rampur. Ammi didn't like the joke but that never stopped Abbu from telling it at every family gathering. Abbu also used to say, Ah, yes, nawabs in the past indefinite tense. Atiya's ancestors, Ammi said, had been higher in the order of nawabs. That's how they found the match, Sara. Abbu, for all his emphasis on reading and learning, privileged lineage and family but, thankfully, Ammi was more practical. Luckily for me, your mother ticked both boxes. Atiya said roughly the same thing about her parents but in the reverse order, and was relieved that I 'somehow ticked both boxes too'.

I'll tell Sara, yes, ours was an arranged marriage but

Atiya and I were very much a part of the consultations. And yes, great love is possible in such marriages too. Kids these days, Western kids in particular, probably think it's some kind of insane oppression! I hope Sara doesn't think like that.

Anyhow, Aapa was my maternal grandfather's older sister, who outlived both him and my grandmother. Early in her life, she had decided never to marry, and had gone on to become a revered preacher in the little principality over which her family lorded once upon a time. A pious woman, we were always told. 'It was her personal choice, religion had absolutely nothing to do with it,' Abbu used to say with some kind of cold disapproval.

In my childhood, Aapa used to tell us scary stories when we went to the haveli, or the few times she came to stay with us. We'd sit around her for whole evenings, because along with the stories, she also produced all kinds of unexpected treats from her always-locked iron chest. I loved her stories, which were full of fairies, good and bad djinns, spirits and flying children. She swore that they were all true. Her favourite was the story of the leg that went after bad people. 'If any dirty fellow or impious woman entered the haveli, the resident guardian spirit took the form of a broken leg and ran down the stairs, chasing after the black-hearted guests,' Aapa would say, scanning our faces every time, as we clustered around her. She said the leg was always black.

In the haveli, we, therefore, always moved around in groups or at least in pairs. I never went up the staircase by myself, thinking the leg might appear any second at the next step and come after me. After Nussi, our oldest maternal cousin, said she'd actually seen the leg and it looked like it had tar dripping from the knee, everyone confessed to having seen it. One by one, then, each one of us agreed that your voice dried up completely upon seeing it.

Yes, it does make your tongue freeze, but Aapa didn't tell you that part because she thought you were too young. Nussi confirmed the syndrome. I may have added that it wasn't tar or anything like it, but the blood of the spirit that inhabited or assumed the form of the leg.

—

At some point after we started the special ops in the hospital, I began to see a hand hover in the light of the night lamp. Now, a lot of time has passed since and I suspect maybe I was imagining it, but trust me, it was very real at the time. I have to admit I was frightened a few times. When I shut my eyes, I sensed it waving about in the air. I'm a man of science, Sara, but I'd tremble and feel a deepening chaos in my chest. Then I'd quietly check my blood pressure. On some nights, I turned on another light or went out to the lounge and turned on the TV. Many a time, I looked in the mirror and felt somewhat reassured to see the same man whose face always glowed, as Atiya used to say. I never told her. What could I say? That I'm seeing the ghost of a hand, or ghosts of hands? Imagining things? Trust me on this, one of the few things I'm pleased to have done was my decision not to tell Atiya everything. She would've been even sadder.

As it is, being mostly indoors, reading or watching TV all day, wasn't the best thing, was it? She liked going to the ladies' lunch at the community centre, but that was just once a week.

Oh, yes, she loved that lunch meet. It made her happy. She said it was better than anything she'd seen in India. The group, led by a businesswoman who Atiya had nicknamed The Terminator, had arranged for some catering men to deliver not just an elaborate multinational food cart every Thursday, but anything else the ladies might have ordered the previous week. They played card games and reviewed each other's purchases, sometimes rejecting articles so that they could be returned at the next meet. 'We've *invisibilised* the boys, Kaisu, they're neither allowed to come in nor to speak, just expected to deliver our stuff at the gate and leave quietly with their cheques,' she said one day.

But there wasn't much else that I could do for her. What could I do? I was worried if she went out by herself too often or for too long. You know what I mean.

Sorry, Dad, I don't get that. Surely, everyone went out now and then, Dad. So, no, I don't know what you mean.

11

There was one year when I had to attend to quite a few cases, and suddenly, it felt liberating. Yes, that's the word I was looking for. In that year, more people were in need of an amputation than needed Paracetamol. I felt, well, this is so wide that I can hardly cope. But it also meant that there must be others working to meet the demand. Someone had to do it. If not me, someone else. That was liberating, Sara. It wasn't in my hands, if you understand what I mean, it never was. I was merely a conduit. Even if I left suddenly, the Director would easily find a replacement, and then another. At least, I understood his mind.

And the fact is that they were doing it long before I arrived. It was the system. We merely helped improve and bring it in line with proper clinical practices. That's all.

By this time, I'll have certainly told her that I don't feel shame. It's too deep a thing within me. I was born to do it, my dear, it was prewritten in the lines of my palms. The stars conspired in such a way that I had to end up in Sir Farhad's hospital. During peak times, when I knew there must be others somewhere doing the same thing, a part of me actually felt better. In the hospital, I had a position now, most colleagues gradually came to treat me with some regard, and I had the big boss's ear. There just wasn't much to turn me away, Sara, so I stayed on.

—

You know I'd already lost my home when I left for England, so it didn't matter where I went next, right? And I was always clear about one thing. I didn't want to work in some rundown government rat-hole in India and be happy with the goodwill of people I'd treat for free. In Farhad's town, even though I spent much of my time in the hospital, I was remunerated for everything.

You see, once you lose your home, it's not really recoverable. The only home you have is the lost one, if you know what I mean. Maybe I'm getting a bit soft in my old age, maybe the quiet reflection prescribed for people of my age breeds sentimentality as a side effect, but I do believe home is a place you remember as the site of your childhood scrawls. Even if they have faded, been erased, or painted over a few times. Mine were horses, many, many stick horses. On the ceiling of Abbu and Ammi's bedroom, I'd tried to hide the creatures by drawing on the side of the beam from which the fan hung. I suspect they stayed there until Shabi's wedding, when Abbu decided to have every surface painted over. I had also written on the bit of wall hidden by the cooler in our living room. You know what a cooler is? It's the poor man's air-conditioner. A large fan blows air over a pool of water in a metal container whose sides are covered with real or plastic hay. It can cause dengue fever too, as the Aedes mosquito finds the cooler a rather cosy place to breed. We didn't know it then, we didn't even know what dengue fever was. Anyhow, I was silly enough to think my lines would remain on the wall forever, because no one, not even my parents, knew they were there.

What was I saying?

Yes, I could've built a family home in London—I wanted to—but with whom? The only person in the world who meant home died too soon. I gave up my childhood home when I decided to emigrate, and then I lost the promise of home when Atiya left us. In all this, someone else suffered the greatest loss, without knowing it maybe. And that person was you, Sara. I am so very, very sorry for it.

[I think I shouldn't say 'without knowing it'.]

During a phone call some years ago, it felt like Sara probably thought I don't go out often enough, and in a veiled way she may have wanted to know why. I was puzzled when she alluded to it again in those cryptic letters she sent after her last visit. Teen hormones, I thought. I didn't think she was ready to listen then. I certainly wasn't ready to say all this. I bit my lip and let it be. I did call, but didn't bring up the letters. I didn't want to contest her assumptions. It's bad form. It was a long time ago, anyway. I really do wish she would write again.

Why should I go out, for what purpose, when I'm

perfectly fine indoors? I have a glorious view, although the OXO neon sore ruins it if I happen to look in that direction. Its constant glow maddens me.

And it's not as if I never went out. I used to walk on the South Bank, away from the Waterloo Bridge towards Tower Bridge and beyond. Long uninterrupted walks on new and old pavements, under little bridges, through shabby tunnels that always smelled of urine. I liked looking at the Battersea Power Station. I still do. It's magnificent, is it not? Dark and magnificent. Amidst all the glassy facades that spring up from nowhere in a matter of weeks, it looks like a proper monument. A relic. I like relics.

Trust me when I say this. I love this city. I wouldn't live here if I didn't, but at the same time, I dread this city. It's enormous, it's everywhere, it has too many people, too much movement, too much money. It trembles and rumbles and that, Sara dear, I sometimes find scary. Imagine all this traffic, this *transport,* the trains, the hundreds of metal snakes tearing away underground all day, the cars, the buses, the lorries, the aeroplanes, and the boats that crisscross its earth, water and air. It's terrifying. Better stay indoors, I say. It's much saner.

And I used to go to the pub every evening, well, not every single evening, but often enough to be recognised by Terry and a few regulars. Good man, that Terry, he'd put a 'Reserved' card on the corner sofa by the fireplace for me. It didn't smell of piss there.

Now, I simply don't feel the need to go out much. Maybe I should take up my dear friend on his offer to host me at his 'den in Keraliyam'. Maybe I should finally make the long overdue trip to India and be done with it. Be done with Biju and his curse. Speak with him face to face after all these years—I know he'd love it—and bury my tormentor forever.

Yes, this I must say to Sara. That I'm finally ready to confront that ghost too. To the extent possible, that is, because Mr Biju is really like an undying spell, like an albatross, as they say. Or maybe I've turned him into one by keeping away, by running away, by not acknowledging his existence.

Anyhow, I enjoy this view and the breeze every evening. I walk back and forth in the balcony. Many rounds of eighteen steps if I walk briskly, and twenty-two if I walk at my normal pace, although sometimes the two broken tiles in the middle annoy me. Drink a few small glasses of wine every evening. Listen to music every evening. Remember and forget every evening.

I'll ask Sara to try Billie Holiday again. Oh, that's *so, so* old, Dad, she'll certainly say. I'll play 'Good morning heartache' anyway, and she'll pretend not to be interested. When I play 'Solitude' and Billie goes *I sit in my chair, filled with despair,* she'll probably say, don't go all mushy on me, Dad. You live in a million-dollar flat in the heart of London, remember? Million-pound, I will correct her. Or maybe I'll let it be, it all depends on the moment.

12

In the autumn of my second and last year in England, all the new recruits went on an orientation day. I mean last year then. My love affair with London hasn't been easy, has it? At first, she spurned me. I had to go away, make pots of money, then come back to this ... urban kingdom. They say London will love anyone with a bit of money to splurge. It's true. I don't mind as long as no one bothers me.

Although I was temporary, my boss—Dr Tristan, that is—insisted I come too, which was rather nice of him. They were both nice, actually, him and his wife *Deboraa'h*. We took the morning train to central London. It was my first time on a modern train. It was spacious and sparkling, and its doors shut automatically with a hissing sound; a beautiful female voice from an invisible speaker announced the next station; and the bathroom had fragrant liquid soap and stacks of paper towels. There was a cafeteria at the back, which sold coffee, tea and alcohol. Most people were quiet, reading books or newspapers. A few had magazines too. Across the aisle from me, a thickset middle-aged man gawped at the large breasts of a white woman spread across the full page of a newspaper. I didn't know that newspapers carried such pictures. There were dedicated magazines for all that, I'd thought until then. I was relieved Atiya wasn't with me. She would've been appalled to see such obscenity on open display. I was in a major Western city, I reminded myself, and pretended not to notice, even though it was difficult not to be distracted by a grown-up man with pink balloon-sized breasts on his lap.

[Cut that, Dr K, it's not a good idea to embarrass your daughter with such talk.]

—

You have to imagine my wonder and awe when I first set foot in the BMA's offices in London. You know the BMA, right? Of course you do, of course ... My goodness, the large halls with high ceilings, all those portraits of the pioneers and the greats, those enormous staircases and windows ... Even the curtains contained some mystery, Sara. I couldn't believe my eyes; I was in the presence of medical history! If there was a moment that told me I'd made the right career decision by moving to England, this was it. I memorised the address, so that I could tell Abbu all about it. Tavistock Square, Tavistock Square, I told myself. I felt so sad, so depressed, when many years later I saw on the news that there was a bomb blast on a bus not far from where I'd been on that memorable day. I've heard they rent out some of the halls for parties, wedding receptions and such. Anything for money, the English will do anything for money.

We were to have early dinner at some old club, so

Dr Tristan said perhaps we should have a light lunch in Regent's Park. He had had one of the admin people carry sandwiches, juice and fruit in a basket. The park is something to behold, endless, beautiful, grand, isn't it? I made a note that I must bring Atiya here and I did. As I'd expected, she loved every bit of it and we had a lovely time. I'll tell you about it.

Anyhow, I saw people with very few clothes sleeping on thin sheets or bedsheet-sized towels, white lotion daubed on their backs and faces. In those days, I was surprised to see so many people with sun paint on them. The sun wasn't burning down or anything like that, you see. Just the nice sunlight we get in the winters back home. Really, it was the same kind of warm as our winter sun. If you want to sunbathe and get some vitamin D into your body, which you must, why coat yourself with protective paint, I laughed. Abbu used to wrap himself in a shawl in the kind of sun white people fear might cause sunburn or carcinoma. Of course, Abbu was known for his extreme reactions. I used to love sitting with a book on our little wooden veranda in the winters. There isn't a better siesta to be had than under the November sun in Saharanpur. It's to do with different skin quality, I thought.

We had a perfectly fine time, sometimes laughing at the bonding that the exercises were supposed to inculcate in us, even as I dreaded the moment when it would be my turn to speak. The woman conducting the session went around asking questions she read out from blue or orange cards. I wondered what she had written on my card. I guessed I was orange for temp. I wanted to see, but it was meant to be confidential. I was relieved when the exercise was over. The group broke up. Some of us, including me, lay down on the grass, and a few went towards the massive oaks to smoke. One of the junior doctors—she was Jewish—talked to me, asking me questions about myself, my family, Atiya, and if I missed home. Of course I missed home. Who doesn't? I gathered she was trying to make me feel welcome, which was very nice of her. She offered me some kind of mini chocolates and I ate them all, as I was still a bit hungry. I had never met a Jewish person before, Sara, and I found her to be absolutely normal, ordinary, like everyone else.

When it was time to go, everyone packed their trash in polythene bags, but I couldn't get my hands on one, so I started to look around. The sandwich wrapper and the empty Fresca bottle lay near my feet, I knew. As I couldn't find anything, I thought maybe I should just carry the trash in my hands and drop it in the first dustbin I see. Just as I stood up, Dr Tristan said, Kaiser, we won't leave the trash behind, will we? You see those large bins over there by the hedges? That's where we are going to go, care to join us? I said, of course, sir, of course.

It was later on the train that it occurred to me he hadn't addressed anyone else apart from me. Was it because I was Asian, Indian? Everyone else was new too, and most weren't from London. It's entirely possible that it was a perfectly innocuous thing for him to say to me, but why did I notice it then? Why only me?

13

I THINK I'LL TALK ABOUT Atiya in small doses at first, enough to keep her hooked. I know that's what she'll like the most, listening to me talk about her mother, even if it breaks her heart. Or maybe I should break her heart, so that it's all done and she can get on with her life.

~

Sara, when I first suggested we should probably send you to a boarding school in England or America if you were to have a world-class education, Atiya didn't speak to me for two full days. By now, we had been living over there for about six years. Yes, that's about right.

When I'd said to her in London that we might have to relocate for me to get better-paying work, she had simply said, 'If you think it's good for us, then let's do it, Kaiser, I'm with you.' But, you see, it was different when I decided to take the job, because Ati hadn't been too happy in England either. Or maybe she didn't care either way. Yes, I suppose that's more accurate. Even then, truth be said, I probably knew that if I stuck it out, worked my butt off, then, with luck, I'd probably make it. But I wasn't prepared to be a mule just because I wasn't born here.

Anyhow, at least we'd be among people like us, Atiya had said on the plane, as she rested her head on my shoulder to sleep. I knew she wasn't sure of it, but she said it nonetheless. I wasn't sure either: where exactly were there people like us, in England or over there? If I'm honest, there were, still are, a lot of people like us in Pakistan. These days, and it's a recent feeling, I sometimes wonder whether Ammi–Abbu would've been better off, more prosperous, if, like some of our relatives from Agra, Abbu's father and uncles had chosen Pakistan over India at the time of Azadi. I've heard my distant Agra cousins, Majid and Shahid, are top bankers in Karachi, with mansions, cars and dozens of manservants.

~

As you know, Atiya didn't talk much. I mean, she was the kind of person who often spoke last, waiting for her turn, and rarely uttered an unnecessary word. Early in our marriage, she'd decided to resume her career only after our firstborn, *you*, started school. That was our big plan, that once we had enough savings and you were a bit more grown up and settled in at school, she'd retrain and start teaching again, wherever we were. She loved her work.

Dad, what did she say? Sara is sure to ask.

After I mentioned the boarding school, she gave me the cold stare for a few days. That was her style, an arched eyebrow and silence. I have to say it was much more effective than my speeches. I realised that I'd probably be taking away the one thing that kept her happy. You were content at the local prep and nursery, so I said maybe it doesn't matter where Sara is educated, as long as we make sure she has the right values. Our values. And Atiya said, 'Don't be silly, Kaiser, don't you dare disturb my daughter with values. She's not even three! Let her live a little before she grows up.' It seemed to me she was happy then, or at least not dissatisfied, even though I had a niggling little suspicion that my work wasn't something she could be proud of. She never said a word, though. In those days, I felt she didn't mind it, that she didn't know much, or that she chose not to know too much about it.

I never told her how it all started. I know I should have, but it all happened in such a, how do I say it ... creeping fashion. Yes, that's exactly the word I had in mind. By the time I fully grasped that Sir Farhad wanted Hamad and me to carry on with the job within the job whenever we were needed, it was too late. I never got a chance to explain myself to the only woman I ever loved. It's like a black hole through my heart.

I can't make the same mistake again. That's why I have sworn I'll tell Sara everything, in particular how it all started. The problem is the detail. The problem is I remember a lot and I have to tell her all without going into too much of it. How much detail is enough, and how much is too much? It's hard to tell, isn't it? But narrate I must. Come what may.

Oh yes, there were periods when there was a lull, obviously. Long periods, in fact. I don't really know why. I guess there's a lean period in all trades, and during such times, I was a quieter person. My head didn't feel like a boulder the way it sometimes did before and after ... I felt like I was somehow back in the past. I had time to reflect and I thought it was alright: essentially, all I was required to do was make a *medical judgement,* direct the process, and be there to make sure that the paras didn't mess up like those insensitive imbeciles at Corrections did.

Sara, it was a part of the job and I made enough money, more than enough money. For a responsible family man, financial security comes before everything else, does it not? You will understand when you have a child of your own. I know, I know, all parents say that to their children sometime or the other. But my father never said anything of the sort. In many ways, on most days, as far back as I can recall, he seemed at peace with being poor. He may even have taken some kind of pride in being poor.

~

Then, perhaps because I knew that new cases would arrive at some point, a part of me wanted it to resume as soon as possible. I couldn't cope with the dreadful, suffocating anxiety of the wait. It was strange. Maybe I wanted it to start again because I knew that the long periods of lightness had to end. Does that make any sense? I'm sorry I can't be more certain or clearer.

It was part of the job, I reminded myself now and

again. I bought a new car and saved up. Some might say I could've walked away anytime, but that's just not true. Firstly, I wouldn't get permission to leave so easily—no one did—unless I was on extremely good terms with my employers, and that, my dear, took time, naturally. Secondly, I didn't know I'd be doing it for years. How could I have known? I was no clairvoyant. I was a doctor for god's sake! I am a doctor.

Yes, if I were asked to choose now, if, let's assume, it never happened and I was asked to do it now, I'd, of course, say no. But back then I didn't have much of a choice, did I? I'd been miserable in England. The country made me anxious and forever hesitant. It was cold, damp and dim almost all the time. My shoulders were always hunched. I guess it just wasn't warm enough for my body type. And I didn't have the courage to tell anyone at home that as a fresh doctor I didn't earn enough. I spent almost every penny I earned. It's true. Yes, I sent money to Abbu and Ammi, but that wasn't too much. I worried about our future.

In London, I'd also begun to doubt myself. I'd begun to doubt my competence, my proficiency as a doctor. It's not a very comforting state to be in when you move from job to job, is it? Of course I knew the British health system was stacked against me, and I would have to work extra hard to crack it, pass exam after exam even though I had aced all the tests in India. But that sliver of creeping doubt, my god, it can crush you, finish you off! You may not understand it, Sara, the high achiever you are, but you have no idea how dispiriting it is if, somehow or the other, you're made to feel mediocre or incompetent. I knew I had to get out before I turned into yet another bitter Indian doctor prescribing benzyl chloride in some forgotten practice in some rain-beaten place. In glorious Hull!

Anyhow, once we were there, I thought Atiya was with me and it was all that mattered. Later, both you and your mum were with me and it was all that mattered. I do wonder at times whether we should've returned to London after you were born. You see, Atiya wanted to have you at home, near her mother. 'I'd prefer to scream at the nurses in my own language, mister, what is the point of swearing in English,' she said. 'Urdu, as is universally acknowledged, is a much sweeter tongue.' We did as she wished, of course, but I had another reason too. I wanted to make sure your citizenship was sorted from birth. I wanted to make sure you'd have an umbilical bond with the country of your parents and grandparents. So, you were born in Cantt. Maternity in Meerut. Atiya's family still had some connections and clout in the city. (No one knew mine.) Then you and Atiya stayed in India, between Meerut and Saharanpur, well, mostly Meerut, for a few months, and I flew back to work. What could I do?

~

Should we have returned to London after a few more years of savings? You know, given the city another chance, stayed in it long enough to see if it became better, grew fonder of me. Maybe with time we might have adjusted well, counted ourselves as cosmopolitans, a part of the global village, as they say. I don't know the answer to that, I really don't. All I remember is that, after a few weeks in India, I worried I might lose my job if I didn't go back to Farhad's hospital. People don't get it, but since the money was good, I'd started to feel some kind of attachment to the place. Even though the system ties you down, you begin to depend on it, maybe even like it. Or perhaps it's precisely because of the system that I began to depend on it. Remember, there are always two parties in a relationship, even an abusive one. And back then, there wasn't much conversation about rights, etcetera. Not that the conversation has helped much.

Oh, when I read the Internet these days—only some days actually, as it can get rather tedious—I feel a smile coming, which, I tell myself, I must suppress. Been there, done that. There's quite a bit of anger about that place, and other places like it, on the Internet. Doubt it'll change anything. I have also noticed that we say 'barbaric, medieval' when we talk about the system over there, and merely 'controversial, contested' when it comes to, let's say, your country. This suggests to me that we probably live in a world where amputations and hangings are thought of as brutal, inhumane, but execution by poisoning or by electric grilling of the brain not so much.

Back then, it just seemed normal, and in many ways, it was normal, ordinary. I went to the hospital every day, did everything that was expected of me, and then I came back home. First to my wife, and then to my wife and gorgeous daughter. My life belonged in the house with the two of you, and I was going to do everything to keep it that way. What mattered most was whether your mother was happy. And she was, trust me, or at least that's how it appeared to me then.

~

Well, on second thoughts, yes, Atiya talked to me about it once—just once. 'Are you sure you want to do this?' she said. I don't think I answered. I wasn't sure she knew. For all I knew, she might have been talking about working over there in general. Unless Biju had been talking to her, and she knew some of the details. He could be a proper scoundrel at times. There was obviously more to him than his fixation with restaurants and food.

Do I feel I should've discussed it more with Atiya, confided everything in my wife? I don't know, Sara, I really don't. Now, of course, I'd give anything, *anything*, in return for one chance to tell her everything.

I also do occasionally wish she had talked me out of it, loathed what I did. I wish she had sat me down and said, 'Kaisu, let's go home, let's go back.' I was always more concerned with her disapproval than her approval. She thought the world of me, Sara, so I would have listened to every word. If there's anyone in the world whose word matters to me more than everyone else's, it is hers. But she didn't say anything. Her, how do I describe it ... timid nature wasn't always helpful, even though I understood her personality. Atiya was a gem of a person, Sara, please doesn't misunderstand me. I just felt she needed to be a little more assertive, a little more decisive, if you know what I mean. I had to make all the decisions, and I'm not sure all of them have been right. This, too, I say with the benefit of hindsight, of course.

Or maybe she did try to suggest there was something not quite right with our life but I was too busy adding up the salaries. Maybe she suffered, waned away in silence, and I didn't see it. I have no way of knowing that now, do I? It drives me to madness sometimes, and I drink an extra glass of wine. As I said, I functioned from salary slip to salary slip, coasting along on the bank balance, which swelled every month. It meant I could leave any time I wanted, once I had enough. It meant I could provide the best education, the best of everything, for you. It meant I could provide Atiya with anything once we moved back to England or to India. A fully detached house somewhere leafy. Somewhere posh. Someone to cook for us. Someone to clean the house, perhaps even someone to drive us around. Why not! It wouldn't be a bad life, would it, to have a chauffeur-driven saloon. Another year or so, another couple of years, just one more … That's what fucks up NRIs in the end, isn't it? You see, there wasn't much to spend the money on. Your nursery, and then the primary, were paid for by the hospital. Even when we moved you to the International School, it didn't cost much. You were happy and I told myself that's what mattered above everything else.

Then Atiya died. As calmly as she had lived.

14

Sara hasn't visited for a long time now, but I have a strong feeling she'll come this year. My heart says she will. I'll go to receive her at Heathrow, bring her home in a nice sedan. Or shall I take the tube? On balance, I don't mind it actually, the underground, that is. It's quite reliable, doesn't get stuck in jams, and is quick ... What's more, it's a neat little study of this great city and its people. Oh, but does it smell sometimes! On a busy summer day, it's like a travelling compost heap. Some people don't bathe, and dab deodorant and cologne and god knows what else to mask the stink. Others don't even bother with that. So, god save you if you get stuck in a carriage with no standing room left. Everywhere you turn, you run into volcanic armpits. I used to think maybe it's because some white people don't bathe every day, but then there's no way of telling, is there? And it might be considered racist if I say such a thing, Sara is sure to think so. I don't know much about other big cities, but the London tube carriage is often like a multiracial kit. Yes, goras seldom talk to people like me (even though I've always looked sophisticated, arrived and integrated)—not that they talk much to anyone—but it's still an alright place, the tube. Apart from the stench, as I said.

What was I thinking? Yes, if I bring Sara on the underground, she can learn a little bit about London. Many years ago, I used to notice many well-dressed young people—suits, ties, hats, nice shirts, proper shoes and umbrellas too. I liked it, I have to admit, the effort people made to look presentable.

Now, it isn't as ... how do I say it ... as classy as it used to be. Too many people wear tracksuits and trainers. How do you expect me to take you seriously if you leave home wearing track bottoms, the string bouncing on your groin? An English gentleman in sweat pants. Mashallah. The worst thing I ever saw on the tube on my return was fully grown men keen to show me their butt cracks. I never saw this during my first stint here. And the way these men walk, my goodness, it's a disgrace. Ruined my day once. I wanted to pack my bags there and then and go to India. It's an insane thing: so many men keen to show you the colour and brand of their underwear and their hirsute backsides. Back home, even the poorest of the poor cover themselves, especially in the pelvic region. Even those on the brink of starvation wear a lungi or dhoti.

~

Some may think Sara never speaks with me, but I have video-chatted with her a few times in the last few years. Sometimes, I'm struck with wonder that my little daughter is now a grown-up woman. A smart, attractive, professional woman. The last time we chatted, I couldn't see much of her rooms, though, because it was all curtains. That is all I saw, and it felt to me as if she was looking over her shoulder. It felt to me as if she didn't want anyone to find out she was talking to her father. As though she wanted to keep me a secret. Or maybe it was all in my imagination. Had she not told her friends that she has a father who lives in London? When I bought the apartment, I thought I should be able to host her and her friends when they visit. What use is a three-bed overlooking the Thames if not to entertain your child?

On occasion, I do still wonder whether she's keen at all for anyone to know that I exist. Or does she not want anyone to know who I am, what kind of life I've led? Is she ashamed of me?

That's just not possible. I'm being paranoid, very paranoid; she's my only child, after all. She can always tell her friends, her boyfriend, that I am a doctor. Of course she can. Why would she be ashamed of me! She doesn't know anything, and even if she does have some idea, when I tell her the full story, it will remove all doubt, if that's the case at all. I'm certain of that.

15

AT FIRST, I TRIED TO hide it even from myself.

I mean, I didn't think aloud about it. Don't dwell on it, just don't dwell on it too much, I'd tell myself.

At first, I reasoned that in my profession such moments will, of course, come from time to time, and it's just once or twice a year. A few times at most. Surely, Sir Farhad would get someone else to do this. Surely, he'd have staff trained to do it the humane way. But is that why he'd looked at me, kept looking at me, when I'd finished going on about how ... how harsh their methods were? And that if it was done properly in the first place, the hospital wouldn't have to deal with the mess afterwards.

~

Have I told you Corrections once sent us a boy who looked like he'd been visited by a sloppy torturer? Skin hung from his arm like strips of rotten leather, sickly pus dripped, forming spider threads under his sleeve, and his face wore an expression of unspeakable torment as he walked in. Every few minutes, it seemed to us he was about to faint or die. Hamad and I were both furious. What the hell is this, I shouted, I remember, at which Hamad, god bless him, advised patience.

Many years later, the boy's face came back to me out of nowhere when I saw posters for an exhibition by the artist Edward Munch at the Tate Modern. I looked up Munch on the Internet later and was transfixed by the images.

That boy's face will probably follow me to my dying day. We did everything to help him, fix him and alleviate his pain. I may have felt like hugging him too but, you know, doctor–patient relationship...

~

Yes, it's clear to me that it's like any other surgery, Dr K, Sir Farhad had said. A doctor wouldn't flinch if he had to amputate someone's leg or arm to save their life, would he? My eyebrows must have risen, I'm sure, because he came closer and pressed my shoulder. This was a first. I'd never seen him touch any member of the staff, let alone shake hands or pat shoulders.

This, too, is like saving a life. Trust me, I know. And we have sanction from the highest authorities. I've been striving to make a change here for years, and then you came along. Why should it be done in such a rough manner? Do you not agree? Isn't this one of the reasons we get a bad name?

He spoke softly, warmly, Sara. There was no doubt in my mind that he meant every word. And he truly did. I'm trying to tell it exactly as it was. These are more or less Farhad's precise words:

If we do it the clean way, professionally, it appears to me that it won't be any different from other places in the world. I believe you probably have the same thoughts on the matter, Dr K, don't you? It's nearly the end of the twentieth century, and I've decided to take the lead on this. Someone has to. It's not easy, I'm aware, but I'd like to set an example. Someone has to. We've got to modernise, bring it in line with state-of-the-art procedures. Yes, I'm aware that some come to watch, have a get-together, but only to remind ourselves of our good fortune and the righteous way. I don't quite see how that's different from people who gather behind a glass partition when someone is given the poison injection.

Of course I nodded in approval. How could I not, Sara? Everything he said made perfect sense.

Yes, I wanted to talk to Biju about it at length, but he'd ... he'd become a little too intense in his manner. It felt to me that, because he'd decided that the hospital was a 'stifling place', he proceeded to do things to prove it was so. He wasn't entirely reckless, but he went out of town more often than he used to. I told you about that, didn't I? One day, he told off Zoheb for not being quick enough with his second espresso. Can you believe that?

I told you I wanted a second before you gave me the first, you lazy Bengali, or am I not important enough for you, Biju asked. Then, as usual, he said, sorry, sorry, Zoheb-bai, I didn't mean it, I'm very sorry.

I was in Zoheb's chair, drinking my coffee as he prepared another espresso for Biju who, it seemed to me, was rather desperate to dampen the effects of the previous night's indulgences. This is more or less how he lived in those days: work hard through the week, case after case, eat Atiya's packed lunches whenever she insisted I carry them for him, which was quite often, go out nearly every night, and disappear altogether over the weekend. I began to suspect that he might have somehow started drinking in the middle of the week too. Can you believe that!

The Chief Secretary once hinted that some staff suspected Biju of giving small bribes in the admin section. The CS didn't complain or report Biju; from the way he spoke, it seemed he may have wanted a cut too. A cut of what, I wasn't sure. Biju always had some spare money; he was single, after all, and his folks back home clearly had more than enough; but he didn't have so much cash as to allow him to have the entire staff in his pocket.

Biju was, however, always careful not to neglect his work, I can vouch for that. Even now. I also tried to make myself understand that maybe it was in reality hard for him. Oh, how he smoked at every opportunity during his shifts. I'd see him puffing away outside the door to the parking lot at the back. I knew it was just before or soon after a surgery. God only knows what all he did to his body to stay alert at work. It's one thing to say, oh I can do the job with my eyes closed, and totally another to actually do it, Sara. Isn't it? He was still close to us, the only proper friend I had. Atiya, as I said, was fond of him. I can see that his ... what do I call it ... madness began in the year he started indulging himself more and more. It was around the time Sir Farhad started to pay me extra attention. For all the overseas staff, it must have been a matter of pride that one of them was in the inner circle. But I have to be honest, Sara, and say that I wasn't too sure how Biju felt about it. I found out soon.

When I tried to talk to him about it—Atiya's tiffin came in handy—I made the mistake of first asking how he'd been. I know it was silly of me. I'd seen him only the day before, but you know how it is, I had to say something to start a conversation. Didn't want to abruptly discuss Farhad and his plans for the hospital. But Biju, god only knows the real reason behind his tempestuous moods, he was simply dismissive. Said, look, boss, you and I are different people, with different priorities and different reasons for being here, so how about I mind my business and you mind yours. Please do thank your wife for the food, I do appreciate it. And with that, he left.

~

Anyhow, do you remember the father–son duo I mentioned? They made me think, Sara.

When we did the job on the father, for some reason I imagined him holding his baby son in his hands. I imagined him holding the infant's hand as he took his first steps. The image just flew into my mind. I know, I must've been briefly philosophical, sad, or maudlin ... And when my staff performed on the son, I imagined him not being able to hold his daughter properly from then onwards. I didn't know if he had a daughter. But if he had, or if he were to have one, he wouldn't be able to do all the things his father must have done for him when he was a child. He wouldn't be able to throw her up in the air as many fathers do with their little children.

It was work, but why did I become contemplative then? Why with them? Why not with the others?

The hall, I remember, and I think I've already told you, was very bright. There were lights everywhere. On the ceiling and the walls. As I prepared, the Great Judge sat against cushions on the sofa and jotted down something on the papers in front of him. Four or five people stood around him, looking at the two men behind the glass partition at the other end of the room. I understood that in this town the Great Judge was as important as Sir Farhad, if not more so. I also understood that these two men needed each other, and they needed to keep each other happy. One thing was clear, Sara. Whatever Sir Farhad had planned, whatever his long-term thinking was, it was certainly a huge improvement on the style used in the past. It was literally clinical, Sara, better and most certainly more humane than the methods used in the past.

It occurred to me then that all this was so far removed from Biju's world that he just wouldn't be able to understand anything. He didn't know enough to appreciate what Sir Farhad and I were trying to achieve. That is, if Mr Biju cared to look beyond himself.

Sir Farhad had somehow made me part of a historic change, I felt. He trusted me. He listened to my advice. We had started taking in penal cases the previous year.

Yes, yes, of course, I'll tell you how that came about. You've got to be patient. Please be patient with me.

Anyhow, by now I had a full team of paramedics to assist me. The best equipment. The finest imported equipment. Everything was machine sterilised, as it should be. Sir Farhad had clearly given it a lot of thought. It wasn't some fanciful idea an important man espoused to occupy his mind. How could it be! The arrangements he had made, the discretion he exercised, trust me, spoke of a man who was serious about his work. It was clear to me that he meant to change the system. He had a clear vision. Why would someone make such an effort and spend so much money if he didn't believe in the idea? He was most certainly on the right track, I felt, and if all that was required of me was to supervise the thing once in a while, that was perfectly fine, in order.

I'll say to Sara that I knew it wasn't my home. Those were not my people. And hardly any fragrance ever transported me back home or evoked a childhood memory. But I didn't belong here either.

At least over there I had something in common with Farhad, a shared sense of purpose. He trusted me fully and I trusted him. So, rather than feel uneasy, indecisive, or torn, I should extend all my support, I felt. The Great Judge too would notice my contribution someday. I was sure, although he hadn't looked at me even once.

16

IT WAS THE DARKEST TIME. Still is. Atiya just died—do you remember anything? Without illness, without notice, without saying anything. She just left. For years I've wondered whether it was because she'd had enough, whether she simply couldn't go on, or pretend to go on, any more. Did my wife simply give up on life? On us? You?

I never saw any signs, and every night since then I've wracked my brain, but haven't found any answers. At times, I've imagined another life: that she'd had a serious disease, you know, lymphoma or such, and I cared for her day and night. That I found out early on and I knew how to cure her.

—

You were at school. Atiya called me just as the lunch break finished. Later, I wondered if she'd chosen to wait for the lunch hour to end. It wasn't past the great Atiya Hussain to do that, even when she was in pain.

'It's nothing, really. Don't worry. I'm feeling very tired suddenly. Can you come home early today, if possible?'

'If possible,' she said, 'if possible.'

I wrapped up quickly, requested Hamad to cover for

me, and left for home. Never before had she asked me to come home early. I remember feeling pleased that I was able to do as she wished. She was standing in the doorway between the garage and the house. I touched her face, then checked her pulse, and once inside, her blood pressure.

'You are fine, Ati, what's all this come home early drama? You could've just said you were missing me.'

'I think I felt a little bit of that heaviness again. But if it gets you home early, I don't mind it.'

'But you said you didn't feel it any more ...?'

'Yes, I did, but don't worry, I told you it's nothing. Just a bit of fatigue probably. Can you cook today?'

'Oh, now I get it. All this because you didn't want to cook today, ha ... What shall I cook?'

'I don't know. Think of something. Deciding what to cook is half the job, mister.'

'Okay, okay. Listen, why don't you lie down, rest for a while?'

'Yes, I think I'll just go to the bedroom. It's quieter there. Good night.'

I should've been alarmed then, shouldn't I? My doctor's antenna should have sensed something, don't you think? But how was I to know! She rarely took a daytime nap. In fact, during the years we lived there, I don't remember if she ever did. I felt guilty about it sometimes, because hers was a known siesta family in Old Meerut. 'Where we live', she once said to me, 'every respectable family has a nap-hour after lunch. Radio on low volume, dim light, fan on, and we all go horizontal on the carpet. Greatest thing in life!'

Did she ask for me? Sara might ask.

What would I say to that, because the truth is Atiya didn't ask for her. She just said, Sara will be home soon. So, I guess I'll tell her the truth, even if it may not be to her liking. She's a grown-up woman now, not the little girl she was then.

Atiya used to pick you up from school every day, Sara, so when she went into the bedroom that day, I didn't think I needed to remind her. She knew it'd soon be time.

At around a quarter to three, I knocked on the door to remind her. I heard a rustling sound, so I let her be and went back to the kitchen. I'd diced a mountain of onions for the chicken casserole and I started to fry them. When I didn't hear her come out, I went up again in ten or twelve minutes. The door was still shut. The house was quiet. I was a bit perplexed because it was so unlike her.

Anyhow, I went in to wake her, but she wouldn't wake up, Sara. She just wouldn't wake up. She was cold. The AC and the fan were both on max, so I turned them down. I called her name a few times. It echoed loud in the room, I remember. 'Come on,' I said over and over as I looked at her. Less than an hour ago, she'd been joking with me. And now she refused to respond to her name. The room felt still; the curtains had settled into a softer rhythm; the breeze from the AC carried her fragrance.

I told myself I had to remain calm. She'd wake up any moment now, and give me that crooked smile. I held her head in my lap, then her face in my hands. I tickled her palm and the soles of her feet. Her back was wet, I remember. I lifted her up a bit, making her lean against the headrest. She just sat there like a stone. You were at school.

I can't recall my exact feelings as I went to fetch my stethoscope, just to double check, just to make sure. I'd surely made a mistake. Or maybe this was an elaborate practical joke, I thought, even as I knew she wasn't the kind to play tricks. When I came back, she had skidded down onto my side of the bed, face buried in the cushion. I didn't put the stethoscope on her.

A little later, I don't know how much later, I was on the phone with Biju. There was no one else. He was someone I could rely on, despite his moods. And I have to be honest and say, he did everything. He was like a one-man squad. I remember asking him to have the school people call me if they were reluctant to send you with him. I didn't cry. It's an emergency, tell them that, Bij, it's an emergency. Atiya is no more. Atiya is no more. And I hung up.

~

No, Sara, no, I haven't called you here to cause you pain, but I've never talked to anyone about that day or the days after it, and I don't want to die without telling you. That's all.

When Biju brought you home, I took you upstairs. He said he was going to call the hospital to make arrangements.

I shut the door behind us, and you and I sat with Atiya for some time. For a long time probably.

I made up a lie. I told you Mummy had been ill for a long time, but she'd forbidden me to tell you anything. She wanted you to have good memories of her, I said to you, and that she wanted to spend normal time with you for as long as possible.

You were in shock and you cried. Then you'd fall silent, look at Atiya and start crying again. At one point, you asked if you could touch Mummy, and I said, of course, of course. What else could I say?

Was it right to let a six-year-old child sit beside her dead mother? Was I right to let you touch her body? I don't know, Sara.

I just didn't know what the right thing to do was. I simply couldn't decide, so I let things happen. I'm telling you all this because I never had the chance to tell anyone about the day my wife died. I once mentioned Atiya to Catherine, but she was a bit blunt, a bit too direct. Oh, I'm sorry to hear about it, how did she die, was she young? And I didn't know what to say to her. I didn't want to tell her any more than I had.

Anyhow, I dreaded the moment the ambulance would arrive. It was frightening to wait for it. How was I going to let them take her? Just like that? You sat on her right, at a distance if I remember correctly. You were unbelievably brave, I was aware of that. I sat on Atiya's side of the bed and untangled bits of her hair. I couldn't decide if we needed to change her clothes or put something on top of the olive kurta and trousers she was wearing that day. At one point, I thought maybe I should put her in one of my aprons; that way she'd be fully covered.

Of course I wanted to call someone and ask for advice, Sara, of course! I wanted to, but I couldn't decide who. Her Ammi, mine, her brother or her sister? Or Abbu, who knew all the religious rites that had to be followed? I wished Shabi was with us. She knows how to take charge of a situation. Then I looked at you and decided not to disturb Atiya's body.

When they came to take her, you kissed her. But you did so calmly, as calmly you could. You didn't bawl or scream. You helped me with the chadar we put on her head. We tied it around her forehead in the style she wore it at prayer time.

She was to be given her funeral wash at the hospital, after the post-mortem, Biju whispered in my ear. It felt strange that people Atiya didn't know at all were to bathe her. People I didn't know at all. Never before and never since have I missed home more. I wanted to be with our own people. I wanted to be near Ammi, I remember. I wanted Shabi to take care of you while we dealt with the formalities of the burial. Still, I didn't call them. What would I say? Cowardice doesn't really explain it, Sara. It felt like our essence had been extinguished. I suppose I must've felt hopelessness, some kind of resignation, defeat, which perhaps made me feel, what's the point, it's all over, what's the point of anything?

Years later, when I was home for Abbu's funeral, I told Shabi a bit of what I felt the day Atiya left us. Even then, I couldn't bring myself to describe anything in detail, or give her a full account of what happened and how we felt.

Soon, we were in the ambulance with her. All together. We waited for the post-mortem. I kept you close. At the hospital, you drank a lot of water. It's been more than eighteen years since then, but I remember it like it was yesterday. You kept going to refill your glass at the dispenser. You sat by my side, holding onto to my elbow, and from time to time, you stood up to get water and drank in small sips. Probably hundreds of sips.

The hospital did the post-mortem as a priority. I was a staff member, after all. The consultant said it was a sudden cardiac arrest.

The deceased's heart stopped between 2 p.m. and 2.30 p.m. She has had angina multiple times before.

Biju, Zoheb, you and I went with Atiya to a beautiful graveyard not far from the hospital. It was tree-lined in front, and tall canopies presided over blocks of graves. Hers was already dug and ready. A few local men, staff at the graveyard, unloaded her quickly, buried her quickly. She was no more.

I didn't say anything. I'd probably killed the thought of flying her home before I could fully articulate it. I remember Biju looking at me for some sign. I gave none. I was thinking, did she always have a weak heart and I never knew, never bothered to know? And I was thinking, what will become of you now? What will become of us?

To this day, Sara, to this day, I choke up when I think that we had to bury Atiya without any of our family around. If there was any way to undo it, I would. I would. A couple of years later, Biju said he knew a travel operator in India who did this kind of stuff all the time but he didn't say anything then because I didn't ask and he didn't want to interfere.

It's a void that hasn't stopped darkening. I was a doctor, I am a doctor, and I don't really know why my wife died. Angina, they said, multiple angina ... but it doesn't make any sense ... Atiya was the healthiest person I knew.

Dear Dad,

I hope you're well.

I've been meaning to write for a long time. In fact, I've always written to you: writing, scrapping, amending, abandoning it altogether, piecing it back together. I wanted to write it all, say it all, in one go, so that I could draw from my truest feelings. I made many false starts and abrupt, possibly forced endings, until I decided to go on the train with my notebooks and pens.

I feel fully together on it, in possession of my mind and heart. As the Amtrak chugs and swerves, turning the world into blurs of brown, blue and green, I find the voice I've been waiting for and write continuously, stopping only when my fingers can no longer go on. I write to my Spotify playlist, I call it Calm & Together, have all my meals from the train kitchen and sleep very well. Please don't worry—I know you do—I travel well, in great comfort, fully equipped and prepared, and face no hardship. I now do this once or twice a year, take a long trip across this vast, strange and beautiful country. I've been on the Crescent, the Cascade, the Zephyr and the Starlight ... but now is not the time to describe American trains.

Without further ado, then, Dad.

I was seven years old when Mummy died.

I remember everything. About her, about you, me, about us, our time together, everything, including mum's pasty white face, white as strained curd, when she was no more. It's mostly a blessing to remember things well and only sometimes have I wished God would snatch my capacity to remember.

I had the best childhood, Dad, and I absolutely loved it over there. After that, I didn't have a childhood: it ended at seven. I will come to that later. I have 51 hours, entirely to myself.

It doesn't matter whether our time then really was a happy one, whether or not I really had a fantastic time: all that matters is, I remember it as the most joyful time of my life.

I loved our house, our garden, our car, my room—all of it. It was the perfect family home. And I had the nicest time at school, Dad. It was so awesome, the teachers and the assistants so kind and sweet, the lunch hour a particular delight, as we all sat down to eat in the picnic area. An awesome picnic every day, you might remember too. My friends Fatima, Zoey and Sugra, and Nousha and Roshan and Sunny!

Do you remember how Sunny came home one day with his mum and dad—what were they called? Adithya and Suhini, I think. It was so funny when Sunny dragged them to our house so that I would agree to play with him, let him join the 'secrets group'.

You brought out tea, cakes and biscuits on that silver tray we had, as Mummy sat with Sunny's parents. Later in school, Sunny told everyone that Sara's dad makes tea and cakes, and her mum eats them. In reading class, he whispered to me, 'Is your dad a cake maker like those people on the TV? Does he wear a tall hat?' And I lied to him that yes, my dad's a famous cake maker and he makes the best cakes for me, which wasn't untrue. You used to bake baby cakes for me and Mummy, remember? They were the most delicious things and only once or twice gave me a tummyache.

You'd wear a white apron and start first thing on Sundays. We'd hear you whistle in the kitchen. I was obsessed with *Snow White and the Seven Dwarfs* in those days, and would watch replays until you brought out the cakes. Purple- green- or red-studded petite cakes. Ammi would almost always say, 'Have a bit of lunch, jaan, there'll still be plenty of room for cake,' and I'd say, 'No. I want Dad's cake.'

Correct me if I've got it wrong, added anything, or made it up altogether.

When this train leans or turns along a curve, I can feel my pen pressing forward, as if attempting to write outside the page, and I'm unable to keep up, to see my pen keep pace with my thoughts. I have a comfortable reclining seat and I bring extra cushions, which I stack on the window side so I can lean on them and look at the landscape. Scenic paint-shop vistas give way to ugly scrap-scapes. I do this when I'm very tired, which is usually during the first few hours of the trip. I work a lot during the week, Dad, but please don't worry, I love working hard.

It's surreal how you can be on a fast train, look out a bit, eat and drink, and yet have so much time to read and write. Why I didn't do this before, I do not know—this letter would've got to you much sooner. But now that I'm doing it, I'm going to go on until I finish, until I'm done.

I was saying, those few years are all I have. That

was my entire childhood. At seven, I suddenly grew up or was expected to grow up. You see, I was saying this and I felt it again: the little girl asked to behave all grown-up!

Before all that, it was perfect really, wasn't it? It was the best place in the world, with my whole world in my hands. I was aware I was an only child, and to be honest, I was very pleased to be one. I had you and Mum all to myself. (Someone or something must have looked down askance at this smug child and said, don't be so sure, kid.) I'm not trying to suggest that the idea of a sister or brother did not cross my mind. It did. And if I remember correctly, I'd have preferred a sister given the choice but, essentially, I was perfectly happy to be your only child. At the time, it didn't occur to me that I was going to be a lonely only child for the rest of my life. A properly only child, an all-by-myself child.

I had everything I wanted and I have to thank you for that, Dad. You made sure I never had to ask twice for anything. Sometimes, I'd overhear Ammi say that you were spoiling me, that I had to know there were limits to what I could have. Do you remember what you said to her?

'What if I die tomorrow, Atiya? What good is all the money if I can't spend it on my daughter?'

Later, at the boarding school in America, I often prayed that you would magically come to be with me every day. My dad can get anything in the world if I want it, I'd say to my classmates. When it soon dawned on me that there were rules in the school about what I could and couldn't have, I missed you more. Not for the things, I swear, but for the idea, for the possibility, that if I needed anything, Dad would scour the universe for it.

Over time, I've come to realise that we measure our lives in terms of the things we can't do, and I think it's a sad way to live. Perhaps a necessary but dull, sad way to live life. I have thought about it often: how to exist while counting the things I can't do, I can't have, I can't be! It's a reduced way to live.

~

When I was little, I had a mother and a father and they loved me as dearly as any parent would love their only daughter. Probably even more.

Then I didn't have a mother. I was told she's gone to a better place from where she'd watch over me all my life.

Then you decided to take away my father from me. I was told you had to do so in order to give me a better life: a better and fuller shot at life, and that you'd watch over me all the time.

So, I became an orphan with a mother gone to a better place and a father who sent money all the time so I could have a better life. I guess a well-provided-for orphan is much better than an impoverished orphan.

Please don't misunderstand me, Dad. You believed you did the right thing by packing me off, but has it ever crossed your mind that I might have preferred to stay with my father?

More so because suddenly I didn't have a mother, more so because I've never—not for a single day, not for a moment—been able to forget you and me in the morgue, waiting for Mummy's body to be cleared for next of kin. It's entirely possible that you couldn't and still can't imagine how frightening it was, and how every day since then became a fright: how I keep going back to that day.

I clung to you, dear father, and I felt safer and warmer. Then suddenly I felt very, very dry in my mouth, as if someone had fed me hot soot. So I left your side, terrified as I stood up, my legs quivering, to go and drink some water. I did so quickly, so that I could come back to you and feel your body, breathing and alive, put my arm in your lap, touch my shoulder to your side, and smell the dad smell on you. Perhaps because I was parched with sadness and fear, I went again and again to drink water, but I didn't stand there long enough to fill my body. Because I was scared you might go somewhere or disappear in the meantime. What would I do then? Even when I stood at the dispenser, I tried to sense your presence on the other side of the room with my mind, my heart, my ears.

For months, I didn't want to go to my room, and I panicked when I had to use the bathroom, as it removed you from my sight. Because being with you, being next to you, locking my arm in yours and feeling your pulse, gave me solace and safety.

The waiting room at the morgue was all white—do you remember it?—and we waited, father and daughter, daughter and father, for my mother to be released so she could be away on her final journey.

Maybe what I said earlier was harsh. I'm sure you knew how scared I was, Dad. How could you not? I wanted to run out of that room and yet I knew there was no way Mummy could come back once they brought her out. While we were waiting, and miracles are known to happen during waiting, there was still hope, I must have thought in my mind. But once that large inner door opened, there was only one way to go. Only one destination. For her, and for you and me: the graveyard. Yes, Dad, I knew. How could I not! Perhaps that's why I swallowed all the time, felt a scratchy, prickly dryness in my mouth. The idea, the fact, that they'd bury her soon, put her in a grave, in an Ammi-sized hole in the dry earth and cover her with a mound of earth.

I recall feeling bad for her—that they'd spoil her pristine clothes, fling dirt on them, make stains. I didn't know what a shroud was, Dad, or maybe I knew but didn't think we'd make Ammi wear one.

By the way, do you remember her triangle-shaped prayer-time scarf? Cream colour?

I kept it with me, because it smelled of her, of her body spray, and something else too. Jasmine and citrus and wild flowers, always natural ingredients for my cool mum. The scarf gave that scent for years but only faint occasional whiffs now. I still have it, of course

You and I in the hospital van. At the front, because you didn't want me in the back with her. I heard you whisper to uncle Biju. So caring.

I haven't been able to figure out whether I might have been better off being close to Mum, clasping her hand as you led her to her grave. I'm being totally honest, I don't know. What is better? Glimpses of dead mothers or a proper walk together to the grave? Which is more forgettable? Which requires less therapy?

Here's what I've always wanted to say to you: I never thought I'd leave your side after Mum left us. I believed it was entirely up to me to stay with you as long as I wanted. I was terrified of being alone, scared of being away from you for even a moment, but the idea that I'd be sent away, flung across oceans, never crossed my mind. It was inconceivable then, it is incomprehensible now.

I became an orphan the day you handed me over like a little pet to Uncle Aqil. I think I lost you the day I boarded that flight. Please don't misunderstand. There's far too much you and I have misunderstood or misread over the years, but not any more.

17

THE DRIZZLE ON THE RIVER makes me a tiny bit melancholic. I hope that when Sara gets here, the weather behaves. Oh my god, you're more British than the Brits, Dad, she might say if I mention the weather too often. Ah, I could perhaps retort, you're like, totally like, an American now. But I know I won't.

It, the drizzle, isn't unsightly. More like a faint curtain spread across the river through which I can see buildings and silhouettes on the other side. Flickering lights appear as the evening grows darker. It makes me feel this is a lonely city. I feel sad for its people. Many will have to scamper for shelter if it rains too hard. If you think there aren't poor people in this rich city, you couldn't be more wrong, I'll tell her.

It also reminds me of Catherine, who, I've sometimes suspected, may be a homeless person. I can't ask her. How can I? She's never even hinted. But you see, she's never invited me home, whereas I have cooked for her many times. Don't get me wrong, I like cooking, and obviously, I like her. But does it not strike you as odd that, in the four or five years I have known her, she's always preferred to come to mine as opposed to, you know ...?

That doesn't make her a homeless woman, Dad, Sara might protest.

I know it doesn't. Please don't judge me or scream when I tell you what made me think that she might be.

What is it? Out with it, Dad.

I'm not saying it's always the case, or that she's that way, you know, but sometimes she wears clothes that smell rather odd. It's not a foul or unpleasant smell, but something tells me these are clothes she's been sleeping in, or that she's been sleeping in odd places. The sleeves, the collars and hems have a peculiar sheen to them. It's either that, or she doesn't take a bath very often.

You know that is offensive, Dad! I can't believe you just said that, Sara might say. Kids these days.

It's not offensive, Sara, not in the least. I'm just saying, maybe she doesn't shower often enough.

But that's not what you said.

Oh, come on, let's not be too ... *PC* here. It's just between you and me.

It's still insulting.

Okay, I'm sorry, even though I don't really see how it is so.

Yes, I think it's best to apologise if I end up saying something like that. I may have done so a couple of times in the past, not with Sara, though. Uff, one can't even talk freely these days without being suspected of prejudice, racism and whatnot.

Or maybe I shouldn't say anything at all about Catherine. Yes, maybe I shouldn't. Catherine worries me sometimes. You know, what if she ends up like one of those homeless people on the news? Shivering, nearly dead or already dead in the doorway of an office block? This is a city that makes both homeless people and shelters for homeless people.

If you're so worried about Catherine, why not ask her to move in here, Dad? You've got three double bedrooms.

Well, well, how do I say something like that to her, my dear? It might not be an appropriate thing to say, no?

Don't be silly, Dad. The next time she comes over, you casually say, oh, it's very late now, etcetera, why not just stay here, the guest bedroom's ready ... Go back comfortably tomorrow. That's how you do it.

Yes, Sara, I know the words. I just can't bring myself to say them to her when she's here. In any case, she's disappeared. Haven't seen her in months. Terry, down at the Mongoose, says Cath's done a runner. (I can't tell if he knows more.) He has a strange relationship with Cath. Likes her, but doesn't like her to come to the pub too often. Now he misses her. He's a bit like Biju, you know, reminds me of him sometimes.

Dad, you overthink things, please just talk to her like a normal friend the next time you see her, that's all.

I think Sara's more decisive and clear-headed than her mother was, which, if I'm completely honest, is a big relief.

By the way, Dad, I hope Uncle Biju's well ... Where is he these days? Are you guys in touch? Do you meet?

I'm sure she'll ask about Biju sooner or later, and that presents me with a big problem. I have to admit he was very good with her when she was little. I was glad that in the absence of real uncles and aunts, Sara had the affection of an uncle figure. *Avuncular figure* is what the English might call him. Sometimes I suspect they may have stayed in touch after Sara went off to America, but I've never asked.

I don't know where he is, Sara. Probably keeled over in his bar in Kerala. That's where he went after leaving—you know that, don't you? He'd started picking fights with me, I think I already mentioned that, didn't I? Then he would make up, saying, 'Sorry, yaar, I'm very sorry, yaar … I didn't mean it.' You know how he was, moody, unpredictable, but a great friend nonetheless, a true friend. In fact, the only proper friend I made anywhere after leaving India. Yes, there's Catherine, but she's not a constant, is she?

What did you fight about, Dad? I know you want to talk about him, she might say, although I suspect she wants it more than I do.

I'll tell her a few things, but not too much. I don't want my long overdue conversation with my daughter to become an account of Biju's life and times. I've noticed that, nearly every time I take stock, he threatens to take over. But I don't want this to be his story, for the simple reason that this isn't his story. It's possible that Sara might want me to blurt it all out, talk about everything, you know … It's possible that she's been waiting for it all along, waiting for me to come clean, as they say, but I'm not going to fall for it. In any case, the truth is I couldn't have prevented it. My conscience is clear. It bothers me still, of course, but it wasn't in my hands, was it? He took over my life and I'm not going to allow him to do it again.

Same things as always, Sara, my job, my work, me …

At the time, I felt he was just jealous, which was perhaps understandable. Within a few years, I was making much more money than him or anyone else. Among the migrants, that is. You see, Biju was a man who loved to spend, have a good time, enjoy life, so obviously he envied me. He would pick a fight and the next morning, like a repentant bully, he'd ask for forgiveness, say anything to make up. Atiya used to say Biju's like the querulous little brother I didn't have, so I should behave like the forgiving elder brother. I tried, Sara, I tried, but there were times when I felt something had come over him. He'd become someone else.

~

'You are the professional he wanted, K, don't you understand? You should just stop. It's not our job, boss! Surely, you can tell him that,' he said to me during lunch a month or so after the procedures on the father and son. Once again, I'd brought him food from home.

'He runs this place, Biju, do you want me to go against him? You try doing it.'

'I would never have said yes in the first place, boss, not for anything.'

'Oh, come on, you think I was sent an invitation to accept or decline? It just happened. You know that.'

'Next you'll say they put a gun to your head, blah-blah ...'

'That might have been simpler to deal with. You just don't understand. It's different here. Different rules, different laws, a different system.'

'Yes, yes, go ahead, bring everything into it, go on …'

'You know me well, Biju, this is so unfair. You're supposed to be my friend, not a judge.'

'Do what you want, boss. When you become the leading wicket taker in this province, and Sir Farhad honours you with a gold medal, I'll clap for you. Happy?'

'You're crossing a line, Biju, please stop.'

'Or else …?'

'Nothing. I don't think I can finish my lunch now. You can have mine too. Here. Have fun. I hope you have a good day and a merry time in the Gold City!'

With that I stood up and left. Maybe I shouldn't have said that bit about his entertainment sojourns. But, you see, I still didn't hurt him. It was just one remark, whereas he—he said far too many hurtful things to me. I didn't even ask him to look at the facts, the hard reality. Perhaps I should have.

I should have said, it's easy to climb a pedestal and issue judgements when you've never been in my position. The fact is he wasn't asked to do what I was asked to. The fact is he never had the opportunity. The fact is it never happened to him. Easy for him to say he'd have said no, no, blah-blah-blah. I hated the way he said 'blah-blah' as he tried to mimic my voice. It felt as though he looked down upon me, his closest friend. The fact is that Sir Farhad, as far as I understood, wanted me to be on board, not Biju, not anyone else. The fact is, as an administrator, Sir Farhad was doing his duty, and he wanted it done without fuss, scientifically. In the hospital, we had staff from a few other countries too. Azerbaijan, the Philippines,

Malaysia, Lebanon, Pakistan, South Africa, Ukraine ... But none of them was considered for the job. I suppose the management had decided they wanted an Indian doctor. It was easy for Biju to lecture me, to take the moral high ground. I would've liked to see him refuse the job had he been an A&E specialist.

But he said he would never have done it, Sara might say.

Yes, so he did, but you see, he was never tested, was he? And I can tell you he wasn't exactly the upright, honest gentleman he claimed to be. He would've sold his mother for a drink in the Gold City.

But aren't those two different things, Dad?

Yes, yes, vastly different. What I did was a part of my job, for which I was paid a good salary, which paid for...

That is some consolation.

Are you being ironic?

Never, Dad, never.

I was only teasing you, Sara. May God bless you. Look, I may have felt hurt, because Atiya and I were always nice to him. Atiya often packed extra food when I carried lunch to work. 'Your friend is kind of tiny but, Mashallah, can he eat. Where does it all go?' She joked about Biju's appetite almost every time. The first or the second time we had him over for dinner, Atiya had to try hard not to laugh at the mountain of rice and karahi chicken Biju deposited on his plate. She covered her mouth as the pile of food disappeared down Biju's mouth. Indeed, it was as if he had a well in place of a stomach.

Anyhow, enough about him. I don't want to talk about him any more! He could be so petty sometimes.

Do you know what he said to me once, after I'd been to Corrections? This was before the whole thing was shifted to the hospital.

'You are at the cutting edge of your profession, Dr K, congratulations.' It was so callous of him. I don't want to talk about it any more.

18

Sara, look, I didn't exactly intend to be where I am today. Yes, I'd dreamt of moving back here, buying a house somewhere nice. Yes, that part I intended, and by the time I decided to retire early, I knew I wanted to live in London. As far as I'm concerned, there are only two parts to England, you could even say two countries: London and the rest. My first attempt at courting the city wasn't exactly grand, was it?

I'd dreamt of a life together with Atiya and you. In a sought-after part of the city, but a nice suburb would be fine too. Cockfosters probably, where the rich and the retired live. Or maybe not. I went there once to look at a former stables that was on sale, and found the area rather, uh, anodyne, you know, a bit lifeless. It's green and beautiful and all that, but I didn't feel the buzz of life. Of course, the mistake was entirely mine. What *buzz* would I feel in a spare-cash suburb? I guess they prefer to stay in their indoor pools or home cinemas or tanning rooms. The stables, which the estate agent had advertised as a 'period property with splendid room for improvement', were a dump. Period features meant an old broken-down fireplace and a few rusted iron pegs poking out of a mud wall. I'm sure they believed they could easily fool an old Indian doctor. Fools. I've come to believe estate agents are a different species altogether, not from planet Earth.

Anyhow, some of the houses in the area, oh my god, they were the kind you see in Hindi films, and the cars, well, fleets of them behind electronic fences.

~

But I lost Atiya, and then you, so even as I could've afforded a house somewhere posh, I chose to buy this apartment instead. A grand and empty house would have reminded me of the dream too often. The reality, however, is that this, too, reminds me of the promises I made to myself. The ones I kept and the ones I didn't and couldn't keep.

I earned a lot of money, my dear, and I saved every pound I could. That's what I did for more than two decades: put money in the bank, put money in the bank.

~

I'd cracked London early, I'll tell her.

This is a city where you are nothing, absolutely nothing, without property—something, anything—to your name, even if your bank owns more than a hundred per cent of it. I figured this out during those first two years here—when the city didn't love me back—that without property to your name, you didn't really exist. That here, your mortgage contract is far more valuable, crucial even, than your nikahnama or birth certificate.

Everywhere I went, people talked about property, houses, square footage, floor plans. Property, property. Two-bed, mid-terrace, end-of-terrace, fully detached, *oh, ours is a corner property, oh, well, mine is a townhouse,* character, period features, original fireplace, Juliet balcony, downstairs WC (why on earth would that be an added attraction?), own back garden (who else's might it be, the Queen's?), fully heated, *oh, ours is in a cul de sac!* Can I be honest and say that Indian and Pakistani doctors are the worst of the lot, all they talk about is three-bed, four-bed, 50-foot loft, electronic gate, sensor lights, illuminated driveway, under-floor heating! In short, I felt this city exists solely for its expensive concrete. And the people in it live to service, to maintain, these properties, and if you happen to own one, be the master of a place, the city gives you more value because you add to the value of one of its many, many already expensive conversions. Then you die.

Property defines everything here, so I knew exactly what to do: own, *possess,* real estate in this great city. If you bring in money, this city loves you. It doesn't matter who you are. It'll embrace you even if you're the scum of the earth, as they say. You could have committed war crimes against the English people, but if you bring in enough pounds, the city will lay out a red carpet and adopt you. If I was on the papers, I felt, if I was listed as an owner in the English system, I'd have a sense of security. I'd be someone. I can't fully explain it, Sara, but I was somehow aware of all this when I was over there. And that's when it occurred to me. That I wouldn't do what many people do. They tie themselves to a bank mortgage, which is like a leash, really. Tied to a mortgage, I'd have just enough room to move around and feel free, but in reality, it'd be a lifelong restriction. It's not financial freedom, far from it. Essentially, I'd service a loan and pay interest to people who already had a lot of money. I wasn't going to fall for this wizardry from the city's money towers, so I decided to wait for my time. That's how I got to own this place, Sara. It took a while but it's hundred per cent bank- and stress-free. I can leave any time I want.

I'm grateful that I had the sense, the financial nous if I may, not to tie myself to a string. It's like a cage, as I said.

—

I lost you for a long time, didn't I? But now you're back. And if you come back for good, I'm speaking theoretically, of course, I promise I'll sell this place. It'll get us enough cash to buy a large house somewhere nice. Highgate, even. It's the funniest postcode in London. Home to some of the most expensive properties in the country, and also to that Marx chap who said all property is theft or something like that. Or maybe it's appropriate he should be buried in the one of the richest boroughs in the country.

Trust me. I know how the market works. In this city, one can always count on the worth of double-glazing. You can have an entire floor to yourself, Sara, and we'll still have money left.

[Should I say this? Or should I wait until the end when I would have told her the whole thing and it's time for her to leave? I'm not entirely sure.]

I understand your need for privacy. Of course I do. Your own space, a life of your own, so we could even have separate set-ups in the house, if you like. I'm not some boring, old-fashioned, paranoid father. You can even have your own kitchen, if you like. Bring home anyone you like, I promise.

Stop it, Dad.

Alright, alright. You can surely bring him over for an introduction. I'd like that a lot. (Even if you want to live with a woman it's fine by me, I should perhaps add, although I'm not entirely sure.) I'll behave well and be a good host. You don't think I'm capable of handling it? I am not like some of those fathers who watch their daughters all the time.

~

Why do you think I sent you away? Surely, you understand why I never let you visit the place where you spent a lot of your childhood. When you have children of your own you'll understand how hard, how devastating, how ... painful it is to wilfully keep your child away. But now you're home and thank god for that.

I understand, Dad, I always have, she might say.

Are you sure, my dear?

Yes, Dad, I understand all your reasons. But have you tried to understand what it was like, what it was really like, for me? If it wasn't for Uncle Aqil ... Alright, I'm not going to say I totally know where I would be, but I wouldn't be where I am now.

Tried to understand? Oh, Sara, oh, dear.

As I said, you'll know when you have a child of your own. Maybe we shouldn't have this conversation until then. As for Uncle Aqil, no doubt he's been brilliant. I'm always the first to acknowledge everything he's done for you, despite his, how do I say this … rather strange views about your father. I would've thanked him personally, but he just wouldn't talk to me about it! I would've repaid some of the small expenses he incurred on your behalf with double interest, but he wouldn't have any of it. You know that. And, you might agree, sometimes his intentions weren't exactly noble, were they? Trying to create a wedge between me and my only child, the only reason I've stayed sane, the raison d'être of my existence, if I may. The only person in the world who matters to me. How can I forget that, Sara? You know, all these years—ever since then—I've been trying to find some release from grief, and you and I both know what would've been the perfect solution. But I resisted it. Not until Sara is an adult, not until she's grown up and become the person she wants to be, will I ask her to come back, I told myself summer after summer, year after year.

You know, soon after you left, almost every night when I returned from work, I'd imagine I was talking to you, telling you all about my work, what went on in the hospital, about my growing role … No, it wasn't sad, Sara. I was a bit lonely, that's all, so it was fine if I talked to my daughter in the evenings. It brought a kind of solace. I talked to you, not Atiya, because she was dead and you were alive; far, far away but alive and well. Anyhow, I talked to you, told you about the hospital, Biju, Zoheb ... Sir Farhad, god bless him, helped me grow in my career. I took on more responsibilities after I stopped doing the other thing. I'd imagine you were home and I was talking to you. I resisted the urge to make it real.

I decided not to tell you any of this then, but I knew you'd understand when I did. I can't say the same for Uncle Aqil, though. He actually tried to sever my bond with you. Can you believe that? What an odd thing to do. If nothing else, he should've remembered blood is always thicker than water. But, as I said, I'm grateful for everything he's done for you. I'm grateful that when I was unable to visit, he was around, and that you could visit them in Atlanta anytime you wanted. And, of course, I'll never forget that he answered the call when I needed him the most, when I just didn't know how to look after you after Atiya...

He was angry, Dad, come on, he'd lost his kid sister. They were very close growing up.

Why do you always take his side?

Not always, Dad, not always. That's just not true. We've hardly ever talked about Uncle Aqil, so you really don't want to say I always take his side.

PART III

19

ANYHOW, YOU WANTED TO KNOW about Biju, didn't you, I'll say to her a few days, or preferably a couple of weeks, into her stay.

Yeah, why not, but only if you want to, she might say.

The problem is, I have no idea how much she knows ... Or, as I said, maybe she knows more than I think she does, and has been waiting for me to come clean. If I knew, I could calibrate Biju's story perfectly, assuming the right amount of knowledge on her part, but I don't, so what the hell, might as well tell her everything—only bit by bit, of course—about what happened. Besides, I did swear to myself that I'd give her an honest account, without censoring anything.

Well, what can I say, Sara. He would hurl taunts at me now and then. Poke fun at me. Not too often, but often enough to make me wary, even full of dread at times. It was like being in school again. He'd crack cheap jokes and call me names. But I knew what he was doing, so I didn't take the bait, except maybe a couple of times. And, you see, I also knew how to deal with him, hit him where it hurt most. And that, my dear, was his belly. I stopped inviting him home for dinner altogether. He retaliated by going to the Gold City even more frequently. I knew what he was trying to tell me. 'I can always pay for good food.' I think it was during those days, yes it was, that Zoheb indicated Biju might be in the habit of ... you know ... going away to spend time in the company of women who inhabit a certain area in big cities. He actually winked. I said that's complete rubbish, and it would be better if he didn't circulate any such gossip about my friend. To be fair to him, Zoheb immediately apologised and crossed his heart.

Anyhow, Biju went away almost every weekend, every holiday, occasionally took days off in the middle of the week, and sometimes he'd come to the hospital straight from the port. I could smell it on him, you know. He would be clean, in fresh clothes, but I could still smell it on him. Despite everything, though, he was a friend, so I tried to warn him. In those days, he was in some kind of manic mood, almost suicidal.

'Listen, if Sir Farhad catches you like this, you'll be gone in the blink of an eye, Biju,' I said to him one day, as we were waiting for coffee. I was behind him.

'Oh, we are still friends, are we? I'm honoured, your highness.'

'Don't start, Biju, please.'

'But what the hell will fatty catch?'

'Keep your voice down, please. You know exactly what I mean. I know where you've been, where you go, Bij!'

'Don't call me that. Only my mother calls me Bij. Where I go, what I do on my time is no one's business. Not his, not yours, not anyone's.'

'Can you keep your voice down, Mr Biju? You'll get us both fired, yaar.'

'I don't care. I might even prefer it. I'll open a restaurant-cum-bar with the severance pay. Fully air-conditioned. It's always been my dream.'

'You won't get severance if you're fired for indiscipline or misconduct. For breaking the law of the land. Don't you know that?'

'What the fuck's wrong with you, K? What misconduct? What law of the land? I went away on a weekend, for fuck's sake. Oh, I know, I know, you are just jealous, aren't you? You haven't even seen a McDonald's in ages, whereas I ... I am living it up. Well, Dr K, this is called living my life. I work hard and I party hard. That's my motto. What you do is so middle-class, so middle-class, that in contrast I feel like I'm in some bohemia.'

'I have a family, mister, many responsibilities, and what's wrong with being middle-class?' I said to him, Sara. I wouldn't let him have a go at me like that. Yes, I tended not to spend too much on going out, etcetera. Please don't think I was a miser. There just weren't many decent places to go to, and the ones I felt Atiya liked were too far, so we went only a few times.

And how could I tell him about my plans? Why should I have? All I ever wanted was to save enough to be able to buy a nice house, give you a comfortable life, put you through university, get you anything you wanted. That was my one and only goal. And there's nothing wrong with being middle-class, what a silly thing to say.

But Biju wouldn't stop. He accused me of having locked up Atiya at home. Can you believe that? That was so harsh, so ... nasty of him. He said, 'You are just a good worker, Kaiser Mian, an obedient, no-balls man.' Sorry.

'You may be a good man, probably even a good professional in some sense, but you're a small human being. A little man from India gone abroad, that's all! A worker bee. Yes, that's it, I get it. You're nothing more than a worker ant. And you know what, you know what, your wife will leave you one day. She'll have had enough and she'll quit. Just like that. Finito. Bye-bye. Your children, ah, they too will leave you. They'll take your money and presents and property, and they'll run as far from you as possible. Mark my words. One day, they'll abandon you, Mr Family Man. Do you know why, do you know why? I'm sure deep down you know, but let me help you out anyway. It's because you don't know what it is to live. You don't know joy. You don't know how to enjoy life. You want to possess life. Own it. You want to take your bank balance everywhere to feel good about yourself, don't you? When was the last time you took your wife and daughter on a holiday? Tell me. I'm sure the answer is never. I won't be surprised if you take your bank statements to the toilet for your reading pleasure. I wonder what you tell your parents. That you're a super-specialist in some top hospital or some fantastic lie like that? Huh. You are a dignified slave, K. Yes, you heard that right. I wonder what your father will make of that when he finds out. Poor soul.'

I remember every word, Sara, because each word felt like a hot scalpel.

At one point, I had to put my hand on his mouth because he was almost hysterical and just wouldn't stop. I had to shut his mouth with my hand, Sara, and maybe I pressed my fingers into his upper lip. I was shocked that he could be so careless, so disrespectful, so ... angry. Something had come over him. It was all the drinking, I was sure, because from then on, he appeared increasingly—how do I describe it—unhinged. What hurt me most was that he dragged my parents, my family into it. I didn't understand why. Atiya had fed him, packed food for him millions of times, urged me to look after him at work, for god's sake. And he was so wrong about me. I do know how to enjoy life. I know what it is to live, don't I! Look at me now.

—

I suppose what rattled me was Biju's attack on my integrity, on my commitment to my family and my work, which meant the same thing in those days. If I worked well, if I worked hard, my family would be happy is all I knew. Growing up, I knew what it was to want, to be actually poor. I grew up in a house of just three rooms—Ammi and Abbu's bedroom, the living room, and one other tiny bedroom that I vacated for Shabi soon after her matric. Until I was in India, I used to sleep in the living room, folding away my bed every morning.

You know, your grandfather, Abbu, was a ruthlessly

honest man. He struggled all his life, reduced himself to a reed, so that his children could receive a good education. That's all he cared about. Not food, not clothes, not houses, cars, or appliances, nothing else but education. Reading and writing is all that matters, he used to say, and would quote hadith about the importance of knowledge and learning. You know the one I'm talking about?

No, I'm not testing you, my dear, just asking. Yes, it's the one that says, seek knowledge even if you have to go as far as China for it. It's metaphorical, of course. I miss the old days sometimes. Everything is so literal these days. One may as well be blind, or better still, deaf.

Abbu was in his fifties when I left for England but he looked like he was seventy years old. The veins on his throat shone. Being a man of very limited means, with a deep sense of dignity, principles and integrity, is like a lifelong punishment, I tell you. His nose already looked so big. Even though we were better off now, and had enough, he still wouldn't allow himself a hearty meal. 'I will get an ache if I eat a second one,' he joked one Eid, as Ammi put out kebabs for us. She'd made scores overnight. Shabi not only ate from Abbu's share but broke off bits from Ammi's too. It was the last Eid I celebrated with the family, all of us together. I was a bit sad, homesick already, because I knew I was about to fly the nest for good. Ammi and Abbu knew too. Ammi was more reluctant than usual to let me go out to meet my friends. 'Why not invite them all home, I've made dozens of shami kebabs,' she said, as if it was an unbeatable proposition. 'Who's going to eat them here—apart from this little witch. Your father won't have more than he likes to, even if fairies serve him, even if it's cooked by chefs from paradise. If only he had seen how we used to eat in the haveli.'

It was that day, on that last Eid at home, that I realised what Abbu had done to himself. He had become so used to denying himself even basic comforts that not eating a full meal had become a norm. Even a minor deviation from it made him panic. Sometimes I thought that maybe his stomach had actually shrunk. It can happen, you know; it's known to happen during famines and to those who go on long hunger strikes or fasts. Bit of a hunger artist, my father. It all made sense to me now. Why he'd be anxious and frightened if Ammi insisted that he attend a wedding, engagement or funeral in the extended family. Why he wore a pained look as the day approached. He rarely ever visited any of our affluent relatives on Eid. His in-laws, minor nobles from the pre-Independence era, as I said—didn't I?—had long given up on him. It used to be a bit of a joke among us. Hey, Abbu, there's a second piece of potato on your plate, what're you going to do now, run out of the house? What if it chases after you, Abbu? Ammi says there are extra rotis in the basket that you must eat. He'd always give us a half smile. That's all. I know it was cruel of us.

When I first sent him money to do repairs and add a bedroom and bathroom to the house, he framed a copy of the demand draft I sent. It was a State Bank of India document. I remember I got it made from a clerk at the SBI branch near Chancery Lane. He was very helpful. I remember seeing the lower half of the draft pasted on the inside of Abbu's cupboard door. I didn't ask him about it.

Abbu used to say there are only two kinds of people in the world: those who can read and those who can't. I saw him suffer all his life so he could make sure my sister and I were on the better side of the divide he'd created for the world.

—

It was futile to tell Biju all this; he came from a well-off family, at least three generations of whom had gone to university. It was easy for him to scoff at the effort I made. I doubt he'd ever known scarcity or seen his father have tea and rusk for lunch. Spoilt drunk brat he was. What did he know of life that he lectured me on how to live? I am literally living it up now, aren't I?

I think Sara will have some sympathy for me. I hope she does.

She will sit feet up, face in her palms, elbows resting on her knees. She should know as much about her family background as possible. Certainly more about her father's side of the family. I don't know how much her uncle has told her about us. I wouldn't blame him if he has, you know, focused more on his and his sister's childhood in the haveli of Rampur.

20

WHY AM I SAYING ALL this to you?

So that you know your roots, so that you know where you come from. So that I, too, remember. As I order groceries from Waitrose—their online thing is called Ocado; don't ask me why, because I don't know—and they're delivered to me in elegant packaging, I must remember too.

~

You may not be able to understand this, Sara, but one of the most unforgettable things in a young man's life is to witness your father, someone you idolise, someone you love, become a little mouse when a creditor knocks.

I was in India, and had just passed with first position from Sardar Patel Government Higher Secondary, had qualified for med school and was already hatching plans to leave. We were having breakfast one day. It was a bright Saturday morning. Outside the kitchen window, our flowerpots were drowning in leaves and flowers. As it was the weekend, Ammi had made parathas. We had two each. Abbu waited for Ammi to finish, so they could eat together. He always did. Poor man, he must've had two or three morsels at most when someone knocked on the outer door. Ammi looked at Abbu, who must have indicated something, because she then quickly left the kitchen and went upstairs. I knew the kind of knock it was. Ammi and Abbu, of course, knew too, but believed we didn't know, and tried their best to keep it that way.

'Yes,' Ammi said after coming back. 'What shall I say?' Abbu went out into the hallway, Ammi followed. 'Tell him I'm in bed with ... high fever ... hmm ... because of jaundice.'

'God forbid, why must you say such a thing ... a curse on that disease!'

'Say it's contagious, and that's why he can't come out. Just go, quickly.'

I was washing my hands at the kitchen sink, which was next to the door, so I heard everything. I wanted to run upstairs, take out cash from my savings box, which I imagined was flooded with 100-rupee notes, throw it at the man who had come calling, and shut the door on such people forever. I wanted to put my hands on Ammi–Abbu's shoulders and bring them in. Shabi was busy gobbling down her parathas dipped in tea, so she didn't witness what I saw next.

Ammi walked back in with her head down and went straight into the kitchen. She stood there clearing up, washing dishes, her back towards us. She didn't ask us to help tidy up, as she often did. Later, during lunch, I think I saw some dampness around her eyes. I felt angry at Abbu. Why didn't he go out himself? Why send your wife out, man? It was like someone challenges you to a fight in the street or at school, and you hide behind your mother. I know it wasn't like that, but at the time it was.

Oh, Sara, why are you curled up like that? You don't have to wear socks indoors unless you want to. We've got under-floor heating.

—

I was seventeen at the time, Sara, and I felt embarrassed by my good father. Can you believe that? 'Tell him I'm in bed with high fever ... because of jaundice.' I've carried that sentence with me ever since and, strangely, I feel relieved to have told you. I've carried the wan bodies of my parents with me all my life, through my migrations and humiliations, struggles and successes. Now, with you here, I can finally bury them. You know, for a long, long time, Ammi and Abbu were both unbelievably thin, not an ounce of fat on them anywhere. They ate leftovers all the time, providing us with the best nutrition they could. They ran themselves into the ground so that we could make something of our lives. I guess it was fine; they chose to do it.

What would Biju understand of life? A carefree little boy at best and a resentful drunk at worst. When I think of that, I don't feel too guilty about what happened. When I remember the things he'd throw at me from time to time, I don't think of him as my great friend. At other times, I feel a shaming sadness. We're still friends.

'I have jaundice, it's contagious,' Abbu said, huh. No, he said, 'Tell him I'm in bed with high fever ... because of jaundice.' I'm not sure why I committed this sentence to memory, but I did. Maybe there was some deeper meaning to it. Maybe Abbu chose the pervasive sickliness of jaundice to convey the overall state of his life and times. Or of the society to which he belonged. The khandani Muslim left with little but a stubborn sense of dignity and pride. Or maybe I'm inventing all kinds of meanings that weren't there then. Maybe we were just, simply put, a poor family. That day, I saw Abbu as a weak man, someone who asked his wife to lie for him because he couldn't face his creditor. Irrespective of what went on in my all-suffering father's head, it has stayed with me, like crow's feet left by a badly stitched wound.

Dad, what happened? We were talking about Uncle Biju!

I know, I know. It reminded me of your grandfather. I don't know why. What would Biju know of life?

You know, now that we're talking about him, Abbu used to feel cold at the mere mention of cold weather. Ammi used to say Abbu can catch a cold if he hears on the news that it's snowed somewhere in the mountains. We'd make fun of him too. And he would make us laugh when we were small. As winter approached, he'd take out his monkey cap and muffler and sometimes chase us on all fours. Shabi used to say Baba Bandar, Baba Bandar, and run off. That means 'Papa Monkey', but it doesn't have the same ring. I think I've inherited that from him, the cold thing, I mean. I hope you haven't told anyone about the jackets. Have you?

Ah, what wouldn't I give to have Abbu here, in this

room, in this house, in the heart of the greatest city in the world? In Central London! How proud would he feel when I turn the heating on with the remote? At least he saw some comfort in his later life. I made sure of that. We all made sure. Ammi once said he'd insist on going to the neighbourhood butcher in the Maruti Suzuki Esteem I bought for them. 'What have you done, Kaisu, your father has gone mad, your money orders have gone to his head, and now the car,' she said on the phone. 'He made me sit with him in the back, gave me half his newspaper, and instructed the driver to drive real slow and careful. '*Akhbar mein bal na padhe*,' he said, according to Ammi. Oh, you don't understand Urdu much, do you? I'm so sorry, it's all my fault. So, Abbu asked his driver to drive so carefully that the newspaper he wanted to read wouldn't get a single crease.

What wouldn't I give to see you and him here together? In the lounge, or sitting with me in the balcony, sipping tea as the Thames glitters beneath us, as London hums and bustles around us. I think he'd cry looking at you, Sara. A doctor in America, he said endlessly in his last months, Shabi told me. My granddaughter is a doctor in America, *a Doctor in America*, he'd tell everyone who came to visit.

What an idea. You and Abbu and Ammi together, over there on the sofa, as I bring out tea and Belgian chocolate biscuits. At first, we shouldn't tell them about the under-floor heating. Won't it be fantastic to see Ammi's reaction to heat rising under her feet? And Abbu, I can imagine his face.

But why did he think I am a doctor, Dad? Sara is sure to ask. Of course she will.

It's a long story. Ammi had become a bit impatient with Abbu towards the end. Snappy, Shabi said, because as his health worsened, he came to depend on Ammi for everything. He just wouldn't allow anyone else near him, even though, by then, we could afford to hire the best day nurse. That must've been trying for Ammi. So, instead of explaining your business studies, Yale, job, etcetera, she just said doctor. Abbu was all for prestige, my dear, all for respect, dignity, and so on. He was an educated man, even if in an old-fashioned sort of way, so I'm sure it was not really difficult for him to appreciate your line of work, or maybe by then his faculties had, how do I say … dimmed. So, probably yes, to shut him up, to keep it short, Ammi just told him you had gone to the States to become a doctor.

How weird is that.

Hmm, not really. He was old and a little bit, how do I say, fuzzy in his last days. Not his sharpest, shall we say. It was hard for Ammi, like always, like most of her married life. By the time I reached Saharanpur, he was gone. So, it wasn't really weird, just easier and simpler to tell him what he wanted to hear.

21

Before Ati left us, before Biju became so unstable, before the special ops at the hospital, before all that, we'd been what I can now, looking back, call content, happy even. If not all the time but certainly a lot of the time. I remember two summers in particular, Sara, one over there, not too long after we arrived, and one here in London, back in the day. Yes, it was possible for us to be happy over there.

~

One summer's day over there, the sky was so clear that for a fraction I felt it wasn't the same sky as yesterday. Atiya had made matar keema the previous night. Maybe it had something to do with the brightness of the day, or the fact that Farhad's sidekick secretary had been hinting about a pay rise for everyone, I asked Atiya if I could have the mince for breakfast too. She was so good, your mum, so good. You have no idea. Sorry. I am sorry.

She spread butter over a slice of bread, put a layer of the mince on it, four near equal discs of cucumber, another slice on top of it all, and said, 'There's more if you like ...'

I doubt Sara will want to talk about anything else

once I start talking about Atiya, our time together, her culinary brilliance, her sense of humour. There won't be any 'what happened with Biju' questions.

'What happened, Dad? Why did you guys stop being friends? Did you make up or not?'

Children these days, such impatience, such short attention spans. Always in a hurry, aren't they?

[Maybe I shouldn't say all this to her. It might upset her. She'll stay for a few weeks, so I'll have plenty of time. Her attention span will grow. In all fairness, though, I know she'd like to know more, wants to know more, about Biju. Sometimes I wish she'd shown the same curiosity about me over the years.]

Even if she persists, and at some point she may press the subject, I can always say yes, my dear, I'll come to it ... It's just that every time I talk about Atiya, I want to recapture it all. No one has made me a sandwich since then, but that's fine; I wouldn't want it any other way. You see, I don't get many chances to talk about her, and I can't talk about her with just about anyone, can I? Only you can understand and appreciate it fully. And right now, I like us, sitting here together like this, remembering her. We must be grateful for our blessings, mustn't we?

Did you know that before we got married, Atiya taught in a government school in Meerut?

Yes, your mum was a trained teacher, Sara, she taught English and history and geography, and everyone liked her. They gave her a nice farewell party when she quit. I went along too and remember we were greeted with massive marigold garlands at the gate. I wore my coffee-brown wedding suit despite Atiya's reservations, while she was in a sari. You look like someone at an election rally, husband, she said in my ear as we waited to be *felicitated*.

Anyhow, Atiya quit the job because she had to move to another town. My town. Not that Saharanpur and Meerut are worlds apart, but Abbu felt it won't be seen favourably in the neighbourhood if she continued to work. 'What will people say? That we are greedy, making our bride commute every day to another city ...' I didn't have the heart to argue with him. But what about Atiya, Abbu, what if she wants to carry on with her job? Shouldn't we ask her? I didn't say any of this. I know I should have. Fortunately, it didn't matter in the end, because a week or so after the wedding, Atiya said, 'We're going to England in the summer, aren't we? So, I've decided I'll spend these few months with the family, mine and yours. What do you think, husband?'

'I think it's a glorious thought, Ati.' I gave her a hug. She laughed.

Oh, you should've seen the way she prepared to come to England. I had to go back to London two weeks after the wedding, I remember. Locum work isn't exactly well paid if you're on a holiday. We wrote letters and she made trunk calls. You have to remember, this was back in the day, when we were a just-married couple. I had no plans to leave England. I loved writing to her. And Atiya said she loved to call an operator at the telephone exchange and ask to be connected to me. 'I am an offspring of nawabs, after all,' she said. I sent her separate demand drafts. From the State Bank of India near Chancery Lane.

I didn't want to put her in a situation where she'd have to ask Abbu for money. Besides, he was a bit stingy, if I'm honest. A lifetime of thrift, you see. DO NOT SPEND had probably entered his DNA by the time he was fifty.

Luckily, Atiya's visa came soon. In those days, it wasn't too complicated. It was a much simpler time in many ways. Brits still needed lots of people to work in hospitals, construction, airports, hotel kitchens and, of course, in curry houses. It's another matter how some of us felt when we arrived.

Anyhow, four or five months after our wedding, Atiya arrived with a suitcase in her hand and a dark purple chadar on her head. She looked gorgeous in her salwar kameez and the long coat over it. In her hand, she held the purse she'd carried on our wedding day. It was a family heirloom, given to her by her mother, who had inherited it from her mother. 'Finally some proof that your forefathers were nobles,' I'd joked on our wedding night when at last she made it to our over-decorated room after dozens of rituals in the house.

At Heathrow, I tried to hug her, but she flinched. She was a bit scared, almost talking in a whisper. If there was ever a flaw in her, it was her ... reticence. Yes, that's the word I was looking for. She just couldn't assert herself or make her presence felt in new places. In those days, the few times we socialised, she'd hide behind me or lurk around the furniture. Not that I took her to any fancy gatherings. I didn't know any. Some of those—only some, I insist—who had arrived the last year or the year before, hosted dinners for those who had just landed. (There was, and probably still is, a hierarchy among the arrivees.) Getting to know each other or, if I'm honest, locum network dinners and such. Even at these functions, Atiya preferred to stay close to me rather than talk to new people. I have to admit I was a tiny bit frustrated sometimes. Many of the freshie wives couldn't speak English properly but your mum spoke fluently, and yet, she shied away from people. It frustrated me but I loved her, Sara, so I never pushed her. It's the truth. What was the point, right? She spoke more freely with Bala and her husband, oho, that's the Tamil couple who ran the corner-store, and the few waiters we began to recognise at Indian restaurants. Can you believe that? That was your amazing-amazing mum, asking waiters about their families, career and marriage plans, if they were treated well, if they were happy...

Goodness, the first time we had what the Brits call a curry was some revelation. I still remember the restaurant near Walthamstow. *Pearl of India, Est. 1965, Fully Air-Conditioned.* It was nothing like our food, trust me. All I saw was flakes of red paint and cream floating on top of shoddily cut pieces of meat. Who puts raw cream in rogan josh? Indian Restaurants run by Enterprising Bangladeshis for White People in East London. That's who.

Then again, Indian restaurants and Regent's Park and the mosque there were probably the only places where she felt perfectly comfortable, so we went every weekend and on some Fridays—basically whenever I could. She loved going to the restaurants, and I adored the way she got ready.

—

At the picnic after Friday prayers in Regent's Park once, we played Frisbee. Atiya's chadar fluttered like a mast as she ran to catch. What a beautiful day it was, what a marvellous day, if I may. She was good at it, much better than I was, I must say.

'You're like a national flag on legs, madam-jee,' I said as she caught and flung the Frisbee back with a flourish.

'And you are like a small electricity pylon ...'

Within two months or so, I had at least found a few things that made her happy. Fridays. Regent's Park. Picnic. Frisbee. Bad Indian restaurants. Waiters from India.

As I said, we were happy that summer. By the end of the next autumn, we'd moved.

'If you think it's good for your career, let's do it.' That's all she said when I first mentioned the idea.

In many ways, Sara, Atiya was a much better person than I am. She was clear of mind, honest to the core, wise and considerate. She supported me unconditionally. She was a first-rate cook. Her English was more fluent than mine was then—when she chose to speak, that is. She was ace at Frisbee.

'I doubt you've ever had what I made today. Take a guess?' she said as we sat down on the patch of lawn near the mosque.

'I can't catch my breath, your highness. How will I guess what you've hidden in your basket?'

'You've become boring after coming to Britannia, Dr Kaiser.'

'And you have started calling your husband boring after coming to Britannia.'

'You're breathless because you lost.'

'So I did. You are the Frisbee champion of Meerut, after all. Or was it the royal sport of your ancestors, the other-other Nawabs of Rampur, madam?'

'No, sir, it's the only thing a decent woman from a decent family can play in this country without having to wear strange costumes.'

She took out triangular sandwiches. I didn't even know when she'd made them, and I felt a bit ashamed. Anyhow, I remember the day because the sky was such a striking blue, as though it were new, and I thought to myself, we never get such azure skies back home. It was a sunny, happy day, and we ate mince sandwiches and drank orange squash near giant boughs weighed down with flowers.

English gardens, uff, there's nothing like them. Have you ever been to the Kew Gardens? Oh my god, Sara, you must. It's something to behold, isn't it, an entire cosmos of plants and leaves and flowers. Don't worry, I'll take you there. We can have a picnic day like Atiya and I used to. I can't match the mince sandwiches that she invented, but we can always make do with sandwiches from Waitrose, what do you say?

22

A few years later, over there, as I had mince toast for breakfast, I didn't immediately think of our picnics in Regent's Park. My mind was elsewhere. You were a little over three years old then, yes, and had just started prep school.

What kind of raise would I get? Surely a little more than the others? I should also get a promotion at some point, I thought, and left for work. I looked at the sky again and thought it was probably going to be one of those 'hottest days of the year'.

I hadn't looked up the cleaning staff for months now. Zoheb said admin had recently suspended three maintenance staff for sleeping in one of the hospital bathrooms. They'd been working overtime, decided to rest under the air conditioning and had fallen asleep. They were all Jan's friends. I'd told myself I must raise the matter with Sir Farhad when I got a chance but, one, I forgot about it, and, two, I hadn't been to his office for weeks.

By now, the hospital was taking in punishment cases as a matter of routine, in that whenever someone's time at Corrections was up, we'd be sent a notice. Basically, it was a form Abdel Hamad insisted Corrections fill in every time they wanted to, or had to, send someone to our care. Preferably a month, or at least a week or so, before the procedure. Hamad used a pad of forms meant for use in the mortuary. He had Assad from admin black out the 'Cause of Expiry' column on all the sheets. Thankfully, I never had to look at the forms. Hamad had said he'd look after all the paperwork, which basically meant he'd get Sujo to do it for him. We must keep a record of it, Dr Kaiser, and the families something to bring back with them should there be any complications. Not that there are likely to be any complications; you and I have a neat hand, Dr Kasier, a deft touch, they tell me. Abdel Hamad was probably the only one who addressed me by my proper name, as opposed to the weird habit of using just the first letter. I suppose someone had heard Sir Farhad say 'K', and decided it was fashionable. And once Mr Popular Biju started using it, there was no chance of escape from the disease. Excuse me, ladies and gents, how about you check with me, I wanted to ask.

Just before lunch that day, Farhad sent for me. It could be about the raise, I thought, or maybe about a case he'd like me to pay particular attention to, something he asked of me occasionally, and something I always agreed to immediately. What else could one say, Sara? Anyhow, it had been quiet for a while, so I wasn't particularly taxed.

Before I could make any conversation, before I could even finish my greeting, Sir Farhad said, 'What do you think about putting a partition between where you do it and where we watch it? It appears to me that a reinforced glass wall wouldn't be out of place. What's your opinion?'

I imagined a wall-to-wall glass partition with white light behind it, you know, the kind you see in films. I'd be on the other side, under the lights.

'I think it's a great idea, sir. The room will look better, brighter, and it's also practical, sir,' I said as soon as I saw him looking at me.

'Some of us feel that family, friends and visitors who want to observe can do so without breathing down your or Mr Hamad's neck. It's not a decent thing. Furthermore, even though they are convicts and must bear their punishments with grace, they too deserve some degree of privacy and respect, don't they? Shall we make it glass all the way from top to bottom, or would you prefer a short wall in the lower half and then glass all the way to the ceiling?'

'Do we have to put a wall in the room, sir? I ask because why spoil the space, sir?'

'It doesn't matter. If we need it for something else in the future, we can certainly refurbish it, Dr K. It appears to me that you are not in favour of half-concrete and half-glass? That's it then. I'll have maintenance do it soonest. You'll follow it up.'

'Of course, sir.'

'That will be all, Dr K. You can go now ...'

As I reached the door and turned the handle, he said to my back, 'I signed on fifteen per cent.'

I quickly turned to face him and smiled, I remember. Then I said thank you, sir, thank you, and sprinted back to my cabin.

Oh, yes, I haven't told you, or have I? I had my own office now, with a blue iMac desktop computer and my own water dispenser. They also had green iMacs but I liked blue. Biju must have smouldered with envy.

I didn't go up to check the hall for a few days. Luckily, there weren't any fresh upstairs cases. Neither did I follow it up with admin. They didn't like it when any of us asked questions. I never mentioned this to Sir Farhad.

~

After the holidays that year, there was a drop in the number of everyday cases. Many people were away, visiting relatives, or were gone to the snowy mountains on holiday.

The other cases, however, my cases, suddenly shot up. I learnt later that the Great Judge had passed many a judgement in the weeks and months prior to the summer break, but the city's ruler had decided to defer the punishments until after the holiday period.

Between the adjudicator and the ruler, there was someone who had to act on their system, and that was me or, on occasion, Hamad. I couldn't be the only one. You know who the ruler was, Sara? Maybe he still is.

23

THE FIRST TIME I WENT up to the redecorated theatre was soon after the holidays that year.

'Why can't you stay home for all the holidays, Kaisu? Everyone else must be off,' Atiya had said the night before. Mildly as always. I hadn't told her anything until after dinner on the third day of Eid, when we had Biju over—on Atiya's insistence, I must add. 'He's your only friend. I understand you're upset, and I am with you. He shouldn't have said all those things, but you are older than him. One must always try to mend relationships, not let them turn sour until there's no hope.'

I never said no to Atiya, in case you didn't know, Sara. So, I agreed to have my ... contrarian friend in our house again. He talked to Atiya quite a bit, and only hmm-haan-hmm'ed with me. He told her about his parents in Kerala, and Atiya, delighted as always by the presence of someone from home, listened with undivided attention. I couldn't hear everything because I had to go to the kitchen a few times to warm the rotis and reheat the kebabs.

'My mom and dad are professors, very well known, actually ... Yes, yes, very busy, important people, high-profile members of the civil society too, you know. Someone was always visiting the house for tea, dinner, drinks … Some came just so Mom and Dad would have someone sit at their feet and listen. I couldn't take it any more, Babi. When I was home, I was mostly acting, Babi, acting. Performing the role of the good son of famous people all the time, sometimes twice a day, so one day I just left. I took the first opportunity that I saw and fled.'

'How did you land here?' I heard Atiya ask.

'There isn't a lot to it, actually, Babi. Something smells delicious, hmm … I thought a hospital is a hospital. Working in a hospital is working in a hospital. And I thought knocking out people with a bit of gas is just that, knocking out people with gas. How does it matter where I do it, correct? So, I applied for the first decent overseas vacancy I saw and took the leap, and here I am, about to eat your awesome kebabs.'

He said all this to Atiya, not to me. When he leaned closer to whisper something in her ear, I didn't like it. There was no need for it.

Anyhow, the next morning I apologised to Atiya again and left for the hospital. I'd been meaning to look in on the maintenance men. It had been months since I'd seen any of them. They reminded me of home, of my roots. So, I walked to their quarters at the back and talked to them. They'd spent the Eid eating and resting. And worn new Eid clothes. Only Jan said they'd had a good time. 'We played cards, what else? I won a lot, but we don't play for real, so I returned all the money.'

'Remember the wet cloth, Jan, always remember,' I addressed them all, as I stood up to leave after ten or fifteen minutes.

'Yes, doctor, we will, but don't you worry about us. We are made of stronger skin, much stronger than you chocolate types.'

I wanted to tell Jan that I was hardly the chocolate type, and that for a long time, I'd been the bread-and-butter type like them, but what was the point?

~

The case I handled that day is probably the only time I was rattled, shaken to the bone. I think I lost a little bit of myself that day, I'll tell Sara. It's true.

She was a maid from the Philippines. A domestic help, or naukrani, as we call them in India. She'd been convicted of stealing jewellery from her employer's wife. Classic, isn't it? I was relieved the charge wasn't that of sorcery or adultery.

Our eyes met the moment I entered the showroom. She was slight, without a milligram of fat on her body. She might have been a bit anaemic too. Her wrist was slender like that of a child. It was shining pale and I could see baby hairs on it. My eyes narrowed after making contact. Some tiny hairs stuck to her skin with the ink from the marker and some shone through it. She looked at me, then down.

Outside, Sir Farhad's Chief Secretary, the Great Judge and his retinue, a few officials from Corrections, the maid's employer, who was a tall man in his early sixties probably, and her husband, who worked as a chauffeur for the same couple, sat on sofas and chairs. They watched us perform on her. When I opened my eyes fully, I noticed she'd fainted at some point and my assistants were trying to give her water.

I put my marker down and gave her half a shot of fentanyl. She perked up at some point. No, that's not the proper way to put it. She seemed grateful for the injection and nodded her approval. The migrants of the world understand each other's pains, don't they? I'm sure she knew I had no choice in the matter, but I knew I had it in my power to lessen her pain to the extent possible, and I did, Sara, I did. Her name was Rosie. I often didn't remember the names of patients from the Department of Justice, but hers I do. Her husband told me her name. No, as a matter of fact, he didn't tell me specifically. He referred to her in a low voice when he asked about aftercare. He was relieved it had been a minor charge and, therefore, a minor punishment. I wanted to ask him if she'd really stolen jewellery from their employers, but I wasn't sure if I was ready for either answer. This I didn't know then. Only later at home, as I wondered why I hadn't asked the man, did I realise it.

Rosie of the Philippines left with a boxer's hand, holding on to her husband with her other arm. I saw them off at the gates. I don't know why.

That day, I wrote a short note for Farhad, thanking him for his impressive work with the hall. Only after I'd given it to the CS did I realise that it just wasn't necessary to mention the theatre. I also said that, since it was the holidays and my wife was waiting at home, I was taking the liberty of taking the rest of the day off. Which I did. Atiya hadn't expected me back early, so she was delighted. I wanted to give her a surprise and hold her.

We had a delicious dinner and went to bed early that night.

~

Atiya died soon after.

Yes, Rosie, whose skin was like butter when the blade went in, was the last one I did before her passing. I don't think Atiya knew about her.

~

Dear Dad,

I was nearly eight by the time I started school in America. Uncle Aqil and Auntie Zaynab came to drop me and they did everything to make me comfortable, to make me feel at home. But I knew I was an abandoned girl the moment they said goodbye and I walked into the dorm halls with Miss Kelly. You wouldn't know much about her. Zaynab and Aqil do. She was the one who looked after me and helped me stop crying over every little thing. Some of this may sound like a little girl rambling, Dad, but hey, here's your chance to know your daughter. It was Miss Kelly who'd call Auntie Zaynab for me, but only when it was necessary: when I said I want to go home, and she said, of course, sweetie, of course, your uncle and aunt are going to get you first day of the break, and I said no, I want to go to my daddy's house. Or the time I couldn't get any sleep at night, and I said I want to sleep in Mummy's bed. I know it was childish of me, and I perhaps knew it then too, but that's what happened, that's how it was, how I behaved in those days.

Do you know what I like most about these train trips? It's the idea that the world changes every second. I'm never at one place. It's shifting and leaping all the time, the world outside the window, and I like that. When I've had enough of my room, my stationary existence, my constant, strong and steely self, I start thinking of the train. The hiss and creak of metal running away on metal. I sit by the window and nothing's the same for long. I have no fixed room, no fixed or mapped orientation.

You sent me to an exclusive school, Dad, thank you very much, but I turned out to be an unloved girl. No one really loves you in boarding school. It's not meant to be a place of love but one of instruction and discipline; a place where they give you a template for a full and successful life. And we can say that I am a successful career woman, as we are known sometimes. A successful human being. Full of success.

You will also be pleased to know that I'm now mostly well liked, and Auntie Zaynab likes me a lot too. 'Like my own daughter,' she would often say until one day I politely and deferentially asked her not to say it, because it always took me back to the day when we were waiting in the morgue. We have become friends over the years. She knows me, she knows everything about me, and I don't know much about her life. Dependency does that.

All these years, I have also had a father figure. Uncle Aqil. With whom you don't get along very well, I know.

~

My life so far has had three parts, or, we could say, I have lived my life in three phases so far.

My childhood until the age of seven, when I was full of happiness, I think life with you and Ammi was beautiful.

Do you remember at bath time I always asked for you? Until the very last bath. Not that I had many options towards the end. You were infinitely patient or indulgent: you stood there by the tub doing everything I asked for and when I'd had my full cast of characters in the water with me, you sat there on that aqua blue stool and waited as long as I wanted to stay in, which was more than an hour sometimes.

Ammi would call from the TV lounge, 'Let her be, Kaiser, you don't have to stand there like a sentry. We are just across the door, bhai, just let her be ... How else will she learn?' And you'd always say, 'Just a minute, ma'am, just a minute. There will always be time to learn.'

In the dorm bathrooms, I bathed for two months with cold water because I didn't know how to adjust the complicated shower dial, and I didn't want to ask anyone.

I am conscious that what I'm saying may come across as sentimental, probably border on the trite, but you truly were the best father in the world, Dad, even better than Mummy in terms of time and attention. Mum was brilliant, of course, my absolute darling, and why wouldn't she be? I came from her, a piece of her. I look like her, for god's sake, so she's securely parked inside me, stamped on my face! Drives me mad sometimes, though. But you, you were the parent I wanted to sleep with every night. Do you remember the improbable, crazy tales of djinns, fairies and turquoise-winged 'rocket angels' you told me, as I drifted into sleep? I still remember some, but perhaps now's not the time to recount them. You were the best storyteller-dad I or any girl could have had.

Then you lost it completely and flung me away. Across the oceans, into an alien land where it took me years, until I was fourteen or fifteen, to find my footing, to hear my own voice, and see properly who I was.

I remembered, trained myself to hoard memories, and relived every small thing over and over. These seven years or so constitute the second phase of my life, as I took stock of it, like I'm doing now. It's been a lonely, lips-pursed life, Dad. More in than out. I mostly glared at the world, and didn't make many friends. It's totally possible that I might have come across as cold, forbidding, even hostile.

~

I think one of the biggest mistakes you've ever made was to listen to Uncle Aqil and not visit, apart from those two Christmases when we all got together at Aqil and Zaynab's. When they all got together, and you and I joined in.

You didn't say much then, Dad. Why?

I know I didn't speak much either, but that's how I survived in those days.

You were so very different from the father I knew and loved.

You bought me a laptop for Christmas. It was a Dell, I remember. I used it for years, until it became clunky and crash-prone, and some girls started to make fun of it.

And you gave me money, a fat wad of dollars, and said, 'For emergencies, beta, just keep it somewhere safe, under your mattress probably.' That was perhaps the only time you smiled. Oh no, there was, in fact, another time: when we went for pancakes at Aunty Zaynab's favourite bistro. I hate pancakes, they're the most overrated thing in the world, but almost every time I visited, Zaynab said, let's go gorge on some pancakes, hun, and I didn't have the heart to say no to her. I remember some sauce trickled down your throat and Uncle Aqil quietly handed you a bunch of napkins, pointing to your shirt. 'Oh, oh,' you said, 'I thought I'd make short work of this American roti, who knew they conceal bladders of juice inside.' I felt a bit proud of you for not being embarrassed about it, and for trying to amuse me.

I knew some things but I hadn't made sense of your life yet. What you had been through, what we had been through. You probably didn't know what to say. So, we both looked at each other with knowledge, in the knowledge of–

I guess the overarching feeling, the governing sentiment, for me at the time, was that you had travelled to be with me. You had not been with me for a few years, and then you were with me. You and I together. A bit awkward, somehow retrained or guarded, I do not know, but we were together. You had come to me, for me.

When you left and uncle Aqil decided I shouldn't accompany you guys to the airport, I went dark inside again. I heard whispers again.

But something else happened too, something I can now triumphantly describe as good, positive, and probably life-changing.

You know I found it difficult to make friends, right? I simply couldn't; or people probably found me unwelcoming, closed. After you left, and perhaps because I didn't get a chance to say a proper goodbye, like daughters might say to visiting fathers, I hardened up. I might have even resented Uncle Aqil in those days. I saw him as you, you as him, making life's decisions for me. What is it with men who are so secure in the conviction that they know best what's best for little girls! But mainly, I missed you.

What happened was this, Dad: I started to spend more time in the library. More and more time with books, notebooks, guide books, self-help books, pop-psychology books, inspirational books (this country is full of men who write No. 1 Bestseller inspirational books for other men), poetry too, and of course, supplementary texts for my course work. Say what you like about this country, but they have built vast libraries in their schools and colleges. Millions of books. All kinds of books. So, I spent a lot of time in the library, and I totally loved it. I found my corner, or I created my own, by a large window that looked out into the gardens. The maple, river birch, and elm and magnolia trees outside became perfect silent companions. Beyond the trees, there were a few small artificial hills, each with a fenced-in, solitary treeling at the top.

The assistant librarian, Ms Morton, was exceptionally kind to me: she let me be, allowed me to create my own little space in her domain. We didn't talk much, but every time I saw her, she asked, 'How's your day, honey, need anything?' and then immediately returned to her screen.

The library had everything I needed, including

snacks and drinks, I soon discovered. I felt calmer, less wound up, the muscles on my face less tense. We can say that my confidence grew not in the sports rink, not in the debating club, but in quiet communion with words.

~

I'm not sure you know this precisely, Dad, but the school you and Uncle Aqil or Uncle Aqil and you chose for me, was a top school for 'troubled girls'. They call it a therapeutic school here. Not all of it. I must be accurate in my report: it has a programme, a special wing meant for troubled teens, and I feared I might be joining them at some point. I didn't dare ask anyone, just in case I was supposed to be in the 'pretty block' but had somehow slipped through the net. Please don't get me wrong. Those girls appeared perfectly normal, like I might have, and they had classes with us, mingled with us. But they also had separate classes, and they slept in the beautiful houses reserved for them. I was young, Dad, incapable of a clear sense of discrimination and judgement; I didn't know what to believe and disbelieve.

What was unmistakably true, however, was that theirs was the prettiest part of the campus, with tourist chalet-like buildings, and small ponds and fountains and green squares at the front. I was terrified of it all.

Increasingly, I felt the library kept me from being shifted. If I stayed under, and hid myself in books and manuals and films, I wouldn't be sent to sleep among the troubled. Was I a troubled child? A troubled teen? You wouldn't know much about that, would you? I'd have to ask Auntie Zaynab.

If I sometimes use first names for them, please don't think it's out of disrespect. As I grew older, they occasionally insisted I address them as Zaynab and Aqil, because of which I now sometimes unconsciously use both forms of address. My primal instinct remains Uncle and Auntie.

Of course I suspected there was something to it all: that you and Aqil, Aqil and you, had chosen Riverside for a reason. It was probably the most expensive school in Georgia. In winter, when it snowed, *if* it snowed, it looked like a fairy-tale town with its spires and steep roofs and towers. In spring, a madhouse of flowers. Pink and red and orange and white canopies wherever I looked.

I'd look at the dark knots of the trees outside every day and bury myself in books. Sometimes I think there are only two kinds of people in the world, Dad: those who read and those who don't. I don't know about other people, but I sort of found myself in books. Bit by bit, shade by shade, underlined sentence by underlined sentence, dog-ear by dog-ear, I began to see myself. Independently of everything and, at the same time, in relation to everything. I hope that makes sense. Yeah!

I don't want to romanticise all this, but it's true that it was more the well-stocked library of Riverside than Riverside itself that helped me. If that's what you had in mind when you packed me off like a callous cold-hearted stepfather would.

~

Until then, until I felt the force of words in my hands, coursing through my blood, things had been kept from me. *Things had to be kept from me:* Uncle Biju always corrects and provides a different way of seeing and saying things. He says that's what you were like too, an excavator of language, always digging for the correct word or expression, and that's what drew him to you, or you to him.

Until I saw that books are windows into worlds, I did not know how to make sense of myself, of you, us. Me in the world, and you and me in the world. I could not make any real sense of why I was without father and mother when father lived and lived very well. For a few seasons of doubt, I thought maybe it was precisely because you were doing very well that I had to have an absentee father. I had to be away, with other people, so that my father could do well. Over the years, that has prompted a separate, offshoot question: have you been absent from my life, or is it me who's been missing from your life? Is there a daughter-sized void in your days and nights, in your life and imagination? Or do I have a dad-sized emptiness in my world? So many questions and so few answers.

Why have the other two older men in my life, Aqil and Biju, written to me way more than you have? Or shall I ask why have I, your child, a life form from you and of you, written and spoken less to you than I have to those two?

I want to say something else too. Ask something else too. Do not worry, I'm not going to ask that thing, *the thing*. Not now. Not yet.

Do you know who gave me the gift, the lifebuoy of books and learning? Anything?

Do you know who said that simplistic thing about books and kinds of people in the world? It was Uncle Biju. When I was seven. When Mum died.

Let me not keep going back to that moment, although you and I will have to circle back to that day again and again until we find a new moment to interrogate, to hold on to, to jump ahead to.

But jumping ahead is one of the toughest things for women like me. I have contemplated various jumps and many means of jumping forward in life. They call it moving on. Such a cruel expression.

I have contemplated having children of my own, or at least a child of my own.

I was trying to say there probably is no better or more failsafe way of jumping ahead in time than putting children between yourself and the world. You get old, things slip into the past when you have, see, or meet a child. Yeah, I have thought of it, having a partner, getting married and all. All the things you as my father must fuss about, I hope or hope not, I can't decide for sure. Starting a family, as if it was like starting a new laundry service or launching a new app, entering a new phase of life to put all the other phases behind, at the back of the filing cabinet, and then one day, after I've expended my youth, appear in front of you with my family! With my child, daughter or son, daughters or sons, daughter and son. A husband at the back with the luggage. Your son-in-law. Someone who would join the family, your fold if you like, via me. Yeah, Dad, I have thought of this possible life, but I haven't done anything about it. There may be a man somewhere, most probably here, because I have become used to the rush and push of life here, or there may not. No, I'm not kidding with you. It's the truth of who I am, who I have become. I'm not unhappy and I'm not happy, but despite everything—despite you!—the promise of a future life still does live in me.

I am successful, and for a single person, I make more money than I need, so I give some of it away, and I look good (Mashallah, Mum would've said to pre-empt the evil eye). I have long straight hair like hers, although not as beautiful. I try to keep it the way I imagine she used to, split near equally in the middle with tiny clips on the sides to keep my eyes free of purdah. And I'm tall, as you know.

~

You might remember this other time when I wrote a few letters to you? It's what I feel was the beginning of the third phase of my life, my young life. It came soon after I visited London the last time. How many years have passed since? Many.

I have since left the manic reading-running-cooking routine, and settled into a lifestyle more suited to a successful career woman. Have you ever heard a man described as a successful career man?

24

What can I say, Sara? A lot of the time, it felt day-to-day kind of normal. You may think of it as something profound or soul-crushing, but on most days, everything about it was ordinary. As I said, at the time I didn't think that something I did once in a while, occasionally, could forever be a part of my life. I mean, yes, life changed in that we've never had money issues since, but I worked hard to achieve that, didn't I?

~

Yes, I drifted into it. Well, to some or a large extent anyway. I'm unsure sometimes. I've probably wondered about free will and stuff like that for over two decades, and I'm still unsure. One is never sure about such things. Is there such a thing as free will? There is no such thing as free will. Or maybe there is.

At times, I wonder if killing someone might have been better. There is crime and punishment, a closure of some nature. Now please don't turn away, I didn't kill anyone. I'm just saying, thinking aloud, if I had, might it have been better, clearer cut, without the ambiguity that vexes me? Might it have been better for my soul? I know that, at any given time, the world is full of the sighs of fallen men, but I have no such consolation. I never rose enough to fall.

You may think of it as something extraordinary, but everything about it, certainly at first, was ordinary. Think. They were doing it, they were going to continue doing it and they are still doing it. And not just them; there are people in other places doing all kinds of things to other people in the name of justice ... erm ... medically supervised caning, for example. This country and that country and your country!

I merely helped improve the process, I made it more humane, for god's sake. My presence there was incidental, and it's clear that it had absolutely no bearing on a system in practice for ages. Think.

I'm sorry, I'll tell Sara.

—

You said you wanted to know how it really started, how I got into it, didn't you?

[Oh, to have to second-guess a dear one you haven't met for years and you long to meet every day is like a curse you can't do without.]

Well, to be honest, I am to blame too. To some extent, certainly. You see, as I said, the first couple of years I only worked in Emergency, which suited me fine because I got to learn a lot. Even stuff I wasn't technically qualified to do. I took on work like minor procedures, angiographs, ultrasound, colonoscopy, too—I don't want to bore you—which some consultants, or the seniors, didn't really want to do. I saw it as an opportunity, and in all honesty, radiology was fun. I'd never done it before. Sir Farhad's hospital was a whole world where I'd somehow landed to learn and excel. I was pleased with our decision to leave England. It was unimaginable that anyone in a London hospital would allow me to learn on the job. Not a chance. There were rules even on how to use the bathroom.

Anyhow, I think I've already told you we'd get all kinds of patients in Emergency: minor accidents, people who'd overeaten, domestic workers who took on the hard chores for their masters, young women and men with bruises or concussions, domestic workers with bruises, concussions and fractures, or children who'd been slapped too hard. I once treated a little girl whose left ear oozed streams of pus, because her mother had insisted it would heal on its own. I didn't ask who had hit her. It wasn't my place to ask. Later, however, I realised it was rather hasty of me to conclude she'd been hit. What if she'd been poking her ear, or it had been the result of a fall? An accident, K, an accident, I told myself, and felt embarrassed. Anyhow, the hardest cases were those with imaginary illnesses, fictional diseases. 'It's killing me, doctor,' I'd hear from middle-aged men and women all the time, 'this constant heat in my chest, in my stomach, in my back, my side, do something, doctor, do something.'

I'd prescribe antacid until they came back with another mythical ailment. And the next time, I'd prescribe the same thing in a different form. Oh yes, it would get tiresome.

You know, the only thing worse than a hypochondriac is a hypochondriac with no job. And the only thing worse than a hypochondriac with no job is a hypochondriac with no job and no money issues. He or she will keep coming at you, tearing you down groan by groan, grunt upon grunt, until you come around to their view, and say, yes, you're right, sir, it's a rare, very serious and potentially fatal illness.

—

At the Emergency, we'd occasionally treat people who'd been lashed for something or the other. At first, it was strange and unsettling to look at the lacerations, and a struggle to figure out how to treat them. Mind you, I'm talking about the cases that came to us; I'd no way of knowing whether there were more out there who didn't come to us. I suspect there were.

I observed patterns on flesh. The ugliest scars would be on older men. Uff, ghastly stuff, like embroidery done by man-eating rats. On young bodies, the imprints would be striking, with a strange, exotic beauty to them, like Lucknawi chikan work or block-printing gone spectacularly wrong. Biju, who sometimes filled in for on-leave staff, or was doing overtime to make 'extra bucks', argued it didn't matter how we dressed the wounds, because the scars would remain no matter what. He was like that, in perennial argument mode.

'But we must at least try,' I said one day.

'No, that's pointless, and you're being a sentimental

fool again. It's better to treat them quickly to relieve the pain, yaar, rather than worry about aesthetics.'

'But why not try to do both?'

We were trying to pluck out shreds of linen from the back of a barely conscious patient. Now and then, he mumbled curses, prayers, or a combination of the two.

'Because this man would prefer to have less pain when he comes to fully rather than check how stainless and pretty his back looks.'

Biju was right. I hadn't told him that I'd hoped to learn a little bit about plastic surgery on such cases.

Anyhow, the patient in question was an oral poet or storyteller who had been on a radio show where he recited a monologue consisting solely of a series of questions in verse. Foolish man. He'd been taken away during the broadcast, Abdel Hamad told me later. The poet's back looked like a barbecue grill after the guests have eaten all the sausages and burgers.

And to be completely honest, hardly anyone ever asked if we could do anything about the scars. I think some may even have been proud of them. They carried their trophies on their skin. Like tattoos. I handed out scar-reducing creams, anyway, Sara. How could I not?

So, yes, that's how it went in those early days. You weren't born yet. During that time, that's all I did: minor accidents, and later, some prisoners as well.

Of course, all of it was perfectly normal. What else? There was a system in place. Those who'd committed crimes were sentenced to a range of punishments. Naturally, then, some cases had to be supervised or treated by medical staff.

It's that simple. Someone had to do the job, Sara. Would any proper medical practitioner, a professional, refuse if he was asked to carry out a check-up on someone on death row? It's a legal requirement.

—

What happened was this. I'll tell Sara.

In my second year at the job, one day we were asked to rush to the Department of Corrections to look at a prisoner who'd suddenly taken ill, and the on-duty MO was at a loss. Young man, very good looking, very large dark circles under the eyes. He'd eaten reams of paper.

He wants to be moved to a private room, doesn't want to be with anyone, the interpreter said. I was puzzled that someone would risk his life just to be by himself, or maybe he knew exactly how much paper to ingest to give him a terrible ache and nothing more. Idiot. He had to be given an enema to flush out all the paper. One of the paras joked there was a printing press inside the boy. When I suggested maybe we should be a little more caring and sensitive, the Corrections Officer said it was nothing new. The paras, our assistants, seemed to be in on a joke I clearly didn't understand. Often, the officer said, prisoners do things to themselves or ask a colleague for help, to delay a punishment, to get away from a section they don't like, or just to be with a friend in another wing. Old trick, which works sometimes. Sometimes we let it work and at other times we don't, the officer said.

Yes, yes, I'm getting there. I may not remember the

small details, but this is more or less how it happened. A more or less accurate recollection.

I was about to complete two years at Farhad's hospital. One week, we received a phone call from Corrections. They were bringing in two people with serious injuries. I have to be honest and say I was relieved they didn't ask us to visit again. Every time I was asked to go somewhere, it was stressful. I didn't want to do anything wrong, get on someone's wrong side, you know, and the truth is I didn't want to go too far from home, from Atiya. I felt vulnerable if I went away from the hospital compound. The further away from the mile I had to go, the more adrift I felt.

That day, I was on duty with Abdel Hamad. I'd always meant to ask him why he spelled it as AbdEl and not AbdUl, but I never did. Initially, I didn't like him much. Perhaps he disliked me too at first. I suspect he resented me for being, you know, in the director's good books despite being from India.

As expected, a few security personnel accompanied the injured men. As they brought in the stretchers, I noticed that the two men were alert and appeared to be alright. When they lowered my patient, one of the police officers talked non-stop. 'He's a moron. We asked him not to do anything silly, but he moved every time. It was getting late and our man was getting late for home too, so I said to him, just do it, just do it. Obviously, it wasn't very neat. So, doctor, clean him up, seal it up, do whatever it is that you do to keep people alive. He's bled a lot and two of his fingers aren't fully disengaged, you'd better take care of them too. The Chief said that the hospital was the best place, so we ran here ...'

I was relieved the interpreter kept it short, because the officer didn't seem to be in a good mood and wanted to rant forever, as if he was the one in pain! The interpreter, on the other hand, was thoroughly professional, well-mannered, and respected the doctors.

~

The man's wrist was a mess, a horrible, horrible mess. The only thing missing were a few worms writhing inside his tattered flesh. I didn't know where to start, Sara. And I said to myself. what is this savagery, what is this brutal practice, so unnecessary, and so, how do I describe it ... cruel and stupid? It was brutal. The man who had carried out the punishment—whatever you call him—hadn't done a good job at all. It was amateur, clunky and crude. It was both painful and frustrating to see the man's hand in such a wrecked, raw state. Even if he deserved the punishment, which he most probably did, you owe it to him that there's no more damage to his body than is required. It was practically dripping gangrene, for god's sake.

Or was I wrong? Was it intentional? Did they choose to do it in this manner to make the man suffer for his sins, whatever they were? Did the executor add his own dose to the adjudicator's decree? What am I saying? Punishment for robbery is amputation. Nothing less, nothing more.

Or was it simply an accident, a classic botched surgery? This kind of thing was bound to happen once or twice in this kind of set up, I thought. And why must I single out these people, this province, this administrator? Most certainly it's harsh, but haven't we all been at it for centuries, in one form or another, under one system or another, as per this law or that rule, that other custom? Haven't we always, from the very beginning, done things to people to punish them? Haven't we always devised means to hurt others' bodies? Was this a better way to look at it all? Perhaps.

~

Nonetheless, I told myself losing a hand was punishment enough, why leave a wound that might fester, why cause prolonged suffering, why not do it surgically, cleanly, clinically? Why not cauterise the wound? And why not anaesthetise, for god's sake? What I remember clearly, Sara, is that I was confused, torn and, of course, disturbed. I may even have become furious on seeing the man's splintered wrist again. It looked as if the official who'd wielded the hatchet, knife or cleaver had been intentionally vicious, or perhaps he was trying out various angles. Because how inept could he be? The least they could've done was make clear markings and then a few small incisions just where the radius ends. The law said the hand was to be cut off just below the wrist, not mauled. They do this and then expect us doctors to pick up the pieces. There was no consistency to the system either. Later, much later, I found out they sometimes had doctors on site to watch out for excessive bleeding and sometimes they didn't. In some cases, they didn't cleave off the hand from the wrist, but only took away the fingers, leaving behind a round stump. There was no standard procedure.

Anyhow, I did my best, stitched some veins, closing them, made sure there was no haemorrhaging and, god forbid, any threat of necrosis.

This was, as you might have guessed, much before Sir Farhad built the theatre on the top floor. This was even before Corrections started to bring seriously gone wrong cases regularly to our A&E. It was certainly before I'd any idea, intention, or vision of helping out in Farhad's improvement programme.

It's the simple truth.

25

LET ME GO BACK A little again, Sara, please.

In the early days, every time they messed up at Corrections, we had to rush to the scene. And they did mess up from time to time. I don't think they cared much. Soon, however, I noticed that Hamad was making one elaborate excuse after another to stay behind. So, it was just me and Sujo, the doctor from the Philippines, who went. Often, as I said, it was a simple case of stopping the bleeding. Of course, I believed Hamad at first, but soon realised he'd decided to leave it to the frustratingly quiet Filipino and me.

Thank heavens, death by stoning meant exactly that, death by stoning. Imagine if we, professional doctors, had to attend to people who had been stoned but hadn't died. I shudder at the thought. I shudder. Imagine a menagerie of punishment cases gone wrong.

Those who were lashed.

Those who had to be stoned.

Those who were to be stoned enough to cause them pain and humiliation, but not death.

Those who needed to be beheaded.

Those who must be hanged from a high crane so those who are watching in the circle learn a lesson.

Those who had to let go of their hands or fingers.

I don't recall a single case where someone's eyes had to be gouged out. Thank heavens for that. Did you know that in some places they use chemicals to blind people as punishment for blinding or defacing other people? (I have sometimes wondered if they requisition eye specialists to be on site.)

~

Of course I've thought about those days. Always. How can I not, Sara?

I've asked myself if it was any different from being on the other side of a glass partition in a penitentiary, as our director had said. Was it? Just because they sit with poise, a purse in their lap, as they observe an inmate being sent off on his last journey? [Maybe I shouldn't say this to her. I don't want to upset her unduly.]

I've forever wondered what it all meant generally, and to me and those around me. What it still means. I go round and round. There are no definite answers. I didn't just see that world, I experienced it. I sort of became it, in some sense anyway. Those who turn their faces away, or pretend this sort of stuff didn't happen or doesn't happen are, well, to put it simply, wrong. It's hypocrisy.

We, as in people, have always done this kind of thing to other people, haven't we? We like to watch death, don't we? We are all death voyeurs. I have thought a lot about it, Sara. A lot.

We've always liked to see a killing, a maiming, a beheading, a hanging, an execution, a crucifixion ... Haven't we?

We like to watch people die. It's true, is it not?

We've always liked to look at other people being executed, stoned, caned, shot dead, amputated, put to sleep with a toxic injection, cooked to death in a high-voltage chair. Have we not? I'll certainly say this to her.

~

Did you know that in places where they use the firing squad, one of the officers carries a gun with blanks in it? It's to prevent the officers from knowing that it was their bullet that did the job. Killed the condemned. This introduces a certain element of ambiguity, yes, but I think it serves no real purpose. Each of the officers must go through periods of wrenching doubt. One night they think it was them, and the next day, no, it was the other man. What good is that?

~

Anyhow, in those days, I was the one who was almost always expected to go to Corrections. It felt to me as if I was the only one in the hospital who cared. I began to sense that the rest of the staff who dealt with Corrections didn't think much of it. They certainly didn't care much about the penal cases. It was as if that was another world, a layer of humanity beneath the normal layer. Not part of our world. Or perhaps they thought it was perfectly normal, a part of life, and therefore didn't deserve any special attention. I never understood fully. And yet, all it took for me to be thrown headlong into that world was a call from Corrections.

Soon, I couldn't help thinking about those who didn't receive medical care at all: those who cooperated with the penal system, its judges, its executors, but suffered more than they'd agreed to. Those who were neglected after the event, discarded as damaged goods, or were guilty of neglect themselves. I began to dream of those who were taken to a square and flogged 600 times, or those whose hands were chopped off in a square with a sword or machete. Who dressed their wounds, who prescribed analgesic pills, who applied antiseptic ointment? Who made sure they were safe from infection? You have to understand, my dear, once I was inside the justice system, it was impossible for me not to think of such things. Do you understand? Do you? In the square, it was said that some people not only watched but chanted along too. I gather that nowadays some like to film the proceedings with their smartphones. I'm glad I left before the camera-phone plague hit humankind.

Anyhow, one day I said to my superior, 'Mr Hamad, I'm sure you've thought of this too, sir, but I was wondering, why not bring these people to the hospital before their, you know ... due date? It might make life easier for everyone, don't you think?'

'What do you mean, man? It's not our job, man, not our problem. I know what you mean, but why are you so bothered? Stick to your work, Dr Kaiser. I'll stick to mine.'

'I am talking about our work, Mr Hamad, am I not? Whether we like it or not, whether we want it or not, whether we are asked or not, we do end up cleaning up the mess every time there's a problem. Don't we? There's also the time spent on commuting to and from Corrections. Surely, the management can see the sense in it. They'll also save on the commute and the fuel. Maybe we should think about it, sir.'

'What do you have in mind, man, tell me, but please don't take too long, and keep your voice down, okay? You talk non-stop sometimes.'

I blushed, as I remembered Atiya had said something similar only a few weeks ago. She didn't think I was a chatterbox, but that I didn't talk much for weeks on end and then tended to go on a bit once I started.

Anyhow, I took a deep breath and said to Hamad, 'It's simple, sir. You can tell the management that it's more practical. All they need to do is persuade the Head or Director or Chief of Corrections. If the condemned are transferred to the hospital, it'd save everyone time, and money, and grief. That way, we can supervise the process, direct it and establish correct procedures, meds, anaesthesia, etc., standardise it all, basically.'

I didn't tell him that I'd already sensed it wouldn't be too hard, given that Sir Farhad was the boss. (What I didn't know, however, was that it would all come back to me!) If Sir Farhad was convinced, then whoever was in charge of Corrections would have to agree.

'Good idea, man, good idea. I can certainly supervise you and him.' He nodded towards Sujo who, as often, was updating case files for all of us. Nice man, although I could never pronounce his name properly in the three years he was there. He didn't stay for long.

'But don't get any ideas, man, they'll have to do it in another place, not on my patch. Okay? And we'll choose the staff who'll do it. I'm not doing it myself.'

'Okay, man, I understand. Neither will I, but they'd still be our ops.'

~

Everything went to plan. Everything. Can you believe that?

Sir Farhad was all attention when I mentioned it, Sara. I said Abdel Hamad and I were talking about the burden on Corrections, and we both came up with this small plan.

And he smiled. You see, this was a time when I was still in fresher mode, and didn't think I could have a conversation of equals with the director of the hospital. That was that, I'll tell Sara—and it's more or less the whole truth. The next person due to face the knife at Corrections was brought to the hospital one early morning. All it took was a smile from the big boss. Later, much later actually, I found out Abdel Hamad had spoken to Farhad even before I had.

True to his word, though, Hamad oversaw the first procedure at the hospital. He issued instructions like a pro, and the paras followed every word. I stood next to him. In all honesty, Hamad was always a good A&E surgeon; if only he hadn't been lazy. I don't know if Hamad displayed efficiency because Farhad was around, or because he really wanted to take some responsibility. He was the senior doctor, after all, and my immediate boss.

Everything was so much better than it had been only

a month or so ago when we had to run to another part of the town in a van. I didn't like that one bit. I have to admit that I felt a bit left out when Hamad directed the procedure. I may have even felt a bit envious of him, as I saw him issue instructions in the manner of, let's say, a chief surgeon.

But I had to look at the bigger picture. This was so much better, so much nobler and, how do I say this ... properly clinical. Don't you think?

26

Atiya was pleased when I told her about the promotion. It wasn't untrue, was it? Why else would I be given a fifteen per cent raise? Yes, my role was technically a tiny bit outside of my contract. But it was certainly a valuable role, especially given that I fulfilled my normal responsibilities without any hitches.

I must remember to tell you, Sara, that the other thing was never a daily affair. There were long dry or lean periods. Then suddenly there would arrive a season of judgements, and we'd get busy. Of course, there would be the odd case or two in the middle, but most of the time it was normal work, normal hours, normal patients and normal shifts at the hospital. Routine work. Routine days. Routine life.

[I must reiterate this, just in case she thinks it was my main job. In case she thinks, or has thought so in the past, of her father as some kind of former executioner. Shall I remind her that I never personally carried out the procedures, never wielded the blade myself, or shall I let it be, leave it to her sense of discrimination—I can never be sure?]

It was our third year there, and Atiya was pregnant

with you. We were happy about the extra income; it was very timely. I'd been saving up too. It wasn't a lot, because I sent Abbu money every month, but enough. I wanted Ammi and Abbu to never ever be short of anything. And, of course, I didn't want you to be short of anything in the world. I'd seen the sort of honourable scarcity that men like my father must bear with dignity. I'd seen the swagger of my friends when they rode the new or second-hand scooters and motorcycles their fathers bought them when they joined college. I rode Abbu's painted and polished Atlas bicycle, only on some days, though, I must add, when I was late or needed to get to college early. Its main embarrassing feature was the large carrier Abbu had had put in at the back to ferry things home. Vegetables to beddings, it could hold everything. Poor man's load carrier, Abbu called it.

~

'Do you think they'll let you come with me for the whole three months?' Atiya said one night. I was massaging her legs as she'd been complaining of cramps.

'Hmm, you know that's not possible, Ati, I'm sorry. But I'll join you closer to the due date and stay for a whole month. Badi Ammi—that would be your maternal grandmother, Sara—will be with you all the time. And you'll be home, with all your family, Ati! Ammi and Abbu will also come to see you often.'

'Erm, Kaiser, maybe they shouldn't. Considering their health, we might end up looking after them too ...'

'Yes, I know, and that's why they didn't insist you stay in Saharanpur for the delivery. They'll only come for short visits. I can't say no to them, Ati ... It's their first grandchild too.'

'Okay, I'm sorry ... I'm just concerned that if they fall sick in Meerut, my mother will have three invalids and an infant on her hands.'

'Please don't get anxious, Atiya, please don't. It'll be perfect. Trust me. I'll come for more than a month, okay? I promise. Then, as soon as the baby is travel-ready, we'll all be here together.'

[Maybe I shouldn't tell Sara too much about her childhood. It's bound to make her sad. She didn't see much of Atiya, and later, not much of me either. Well, I didn't have a choice. If, god forbid, I face the same situation again—what am I saying, though, that's not even remotely possible—I'm sure I'll send her away again. Thank god I was wise. It was no place for her, especially after Atiya.]

Can you believe that, that there was a time when we talked about your travel readiness? I assured Atiya that you'd be alright and I knew a few tricks about how to keep babies calm in aeroplanes.

Will Sara ask what she was like as a baby?

If she does, I'll tell her the truth.

You, my dear, were a riot, a one-person demolition force, a screaming, running, jumping banshee, but most often a happy banshee. You had the most radiant smile, like no one else's. And you were so unlike baby girls that Atiya and I would sometimes look at each other and sigh. Then we read books about early childhood, development of babies, gender, etcetera, and learnt it was perfectly normal. You were perfect.

I have to be honest and also say that Atiya and I had probably carried some silly assumptions and what may be called stereotypes with us. We may even have nurtured some subconscious pressure, because some elders, both in Meerut and Saharanpur, had been, how do I say it … rather disappointed that it was a girl. I may have, therefore, felt that you had to be perfect.

What can I say, Sara, it was an older world where a lot of people believed boys were progeny and girls someone else's property.

~

Soon after your birth, as barely disguised disapprovals of our firstborn—*as if*—reached our ears, Atiya lost her famous cool and railed about it a few times. I was the recipient, obviously, but often it was also Shabi, who carried word of who'd said what.

'What's Shabi got to do with it, Ati? These are old-fashioned people who don't know how to watch their mouths. So, calm down, please,' I said to her as she paced the bedroom with you in her arms.

'I know that, mister, but I can at least vent with you here, in my own bedroom, can't I?'

'Of course, of course, I meant you shouldn't get worked up about it. What will baby Sara think? That Mummy has a temper?'

'Baby Sara will have to have a temper and a half if

she is to have her way in this horrible place. Women, I simply cannot believe it—why is it mostly women who are disappointed that it wasn't a boy? Can you believe that? Can you believe that? Our own worst enemies, I'm telling you, our worst enemies.'

'Yes, it's very unfortunate, but please don't be angry. We still have to watch your blood pressure, remember?'

'It's made me so sad, Kaiser. You'd think people in educated families wouldn't have such views, but no, there's no difference between learned honourable Nawab Sahibs and Begums and those who used to bury their girls alive. No better than those Brahmins who give their daughters less nutritious food. I've also heard some actually kill female foetuses!'

'Don't say that, Atiya, please, if someone overhears us, they might think it's apostasy. You're angry, I understand—'

'Wah-wah, wishing that my daughter was a boy, or wasn't born at all, isn't harsh, but my objection to such disgusting views is?'

'That's not what I meant!'

'What did you mean, husband, pray, do tell me, do make me understand?'

'All I'm trying to say is, a few elders have old-fashioned views and it's because they belong to a different time and culture, and we shouldn't be so harsh on them. And people who really matter, your parents, my parents, they're over the moon, as they should be.'

'Well, it's the kind of "old-fashioned" thinking that punishes women for giving birth to a girl. These are the same people who compel women to become childbearing animals, so we keep producing babies until at least one is a boy, and then they blame us for having too many kids! You won't understand, you're a man, you've never faced the barbs or the looks of pity and disapproval, so no, you don't know what it is like ...'

'Arre, how is this my fault now? She's my daughter too.'

'But has anyone suggested to you it would've been better if *it* was your son instead?'

I didn't know what to say, your mum was in such a rage. It felt to me that she'd built up a reservoir of wrath that had burst open. I knew she was right, of course, but I didn't want a scene in the house. It was only a matter of a few days, then the odd relatives would stop visiting and we'd be left alone. That's all I meant. Of course I'd support her if and when needed, but at the time I felt we could avoid trouble. Why make yourself unhappy over old relatives who were going to die soon anyway. I wanted her to remember that most of our relatives were happy for us, as expected; it was just a few strange ones who pissed off your mother.

'No one, isn't that right? It's because you're my husband,' Atiya answered her own question. 'A man. A male. If we'd produced a monster in place of a child, it'd all be my fault, not yours. I'd be the cursed, evil wife who delivered a child people didn't like. You'd be the sad, unfortunate, all-suffering family man, who deserves sympathy and a better, son-producing wife. In all probability, I'd be called a witch: a sinner who deserves to be lynched.'

Never before had I seen Atiya in such a state. Not

before, not since. She is, was, the kind of person you had to lean in to hear clearly. She rarely got angry, but that day, in fact, during those few weeks, uff, I don't know what came over her. She was unstoppable. I was scared for her.

—

When I tell her all this, I'm sure she'll like it. She'll feel proud of her mother. I'll tell her that I was proud of my wife, which is true. Then Sara might feel a bit proud of me too.

After that, Sara, I knew Atiya understood our particular world infinitely better than I did. I felt smug that I'd married her, trust me, I felt fortunate.

Needless to say, we never had any such ugly thoughts. I just didn't think it was wise to pick fights about it. Come on. I was in love with you. And, of course, with your mum too. You were the light of my life. Still are, still are...

Anyhow, Atiya became calmer after a few outbursts, or perhaps, like me, she realised there was no point. I was relieved because I'd been worried about how she'd cope after I went back to the hospital. I worried she might end up killing one of her older aunts with the sheer force of her speeches.

I can't tell you how hard it was to go back alone, and then to wait for you and Atiya to return to me. When you did, we had a welcome dinner party at the house. I put bunting from the main door to your bedroom. (You, of course, rarely slept in it for the first two, no, three years!)

Biju and Zoheb helped a lot, I must say, even though there'd been some cold weather between the two, primarily because Biju was often condescending towards Zoheb. Biju got some catering guys from another town to bring desi food, which he later said was just about alright—passable was the word he used—although I found it delicious, even if it was hotter than I expected.

~

From then on, for a few years at least, life went on smoothly, or perhaps I should say, simply in a straight line. We got busy with you. I knew exactly what to do:

Work hard no matter what.

Stay in the director's good books.

Stay out of trouble.

Respect the system.

Grow in the job and save for our future.

It actually was that simple, and I have to be honest and say I was grateful. We had a perfectly normal time for the next five or six years—with you at the centre of everything, obviously.

Biju remained a source of both friendly support and adversarial discomposure. As I said, I'd sort of learnt, taught myself, how not to fall for his provocations, how not to get exasperated, which meant we didn't argue as often as we used to. I chose to be the one to swallow the bitter pill, and let him say and do what he wanted to. I told myself, if he got into trouble with the bosses, he'd be the one to face the music, although a part of me knew

I'd be there for him. Zoheb once told me we were like a cranky married couple who only met during the day. I gave him the cold stare and he never mentioned it again. Poor man. I hope he's well wherever he is nowadays. I'm sure he is. People like Zoheb are needed everywhere in the world, aren't they? Someone has to turn the machine on. Someone has to make sure it's got enough fuel for tomorrow.

Anyhow, as we grew older, Biju's untrammelled, yes that's exactly the word for it, rants and lectures became rarer and rarer. I didn't rise to the provocations, but I also think we both became less and less combative with time. He was certainly less abrasive, and I seldom gave him the chance. I could see that with age he'd probably turn into someone inclined to sarcasm and wit, but I, or anyone else who had been bruised by his outbursts, would, of course, prefer his wit any day.

By now I also understood I had to make sure I didn't show off my success in the hospital, as I might have done in the past sometimes. It was, in any case, bad form to rub someone's nose in it, and particularly silly because I knew it was bound to make Biju mad. If he was happy or merely content as the A&E anaesthetist, and didn't make any effort to move up the ladder, that was a perfectly normal choice to make. Of course it was silly not to try and enhance your career prospects, wouldn't you agree, but if he chose to stay as a background cog in the machine, who was I to judge him?

PART IV

27

No. I didn't like it. I became used to it, and it became a part of my life, but that doesn't mean I liked it, Sara.

I settled into a rhythm. I know how this may sound but, trust me, I'd already immersed myself in work after Atiya's death, and then, with you gone, there was nothing but work, and work included helping out Corrections from time to time. Even two years after we started taking in cases at the hospital, I felt I must continue to supervise in case a new person messed up. I didn't trust everyone.

With time, people in the hospital began to accord me respect. Some, the non-clinical staff in particular, were in awe of me. I'd done nothing to encourage such behaviour, but I started to notice subtle bows as I walked around Emergency and the affiliated wards.

In a few years, I was one of the senior doctors at the hospital. I was about to complete twelve years there, and my salary was nearly as good as the born & bred seniors.

Sir Farhad started showing a trimmed grey beard. He added two more floors to the hospital. Now and then, foreign specialists came to visit the hospital. Then they'd go off on tours with Sir Farhad. Some more doctors from India, Pakistan and elsewhere arrived over the years. Many stayed on. Some left after two or three years. To each his own, I thought. I also got over Biju's schoolboy antics and his pretentious rants about freedom and rights and dignity. I wanted to say, boss, get a grip on yourself first, then we can chat about loftier things, but I didn't, as I feared it might provoke yet another rant. I left him to his own devices and he left me to mine, mostly. An occasional 'correct, boss?' jibe wasn't too difficult to ignore. I had more important things with which to concern myself.

In the Emergency, I'd some time ago started assigning cases to the junior doctors. I supervised serious ones when they came.

My office was now among the larger ones at the hospital, with an en-suite bathroom. There was a fridge and a television in the room too.

And unbelievable as it may sound, I actually began to have some free time at work, so I read quite a bit. I now also had the Internet on my computer, all of it to myself, so I read everything I could find. I read news about home; UP politics is something out of the world, isn't it! Never a dull moment, as they say. It was fascinating, almost revolutionary that I could read *The Times of India* Lucknow Edition so far away from Lucknow. I also read papers on penal systems, discursive articles on capital and corporal punishment, both for and against, I read about euthanasia for the first time, research papers on medical ethics in Western countries, etcetera; I was particularly struck by the long-drawn out arguments about the role of major pharma corporations in the American penal world. Can you believe that a large pharmaceuticals company, probably Glaxo or Pfizer or Meyer or whatever, I don't remember which precisely, had actually hired lawyers, ethicists and philosophers to determine whether they should continue supplying drugs (barbiturates, essentially, I don't want to bore you) that are used in death penalty cases in parts of America. They call them Execution Cocktails. As if those on death row are offered a basket of flavours from which to choose. Margarita, Bloody Mary, Cobra's Fangs or Pentobarbital moonshine?

At least the ancients gave Socrates the choice to drink it by himself, not tie him down with leather and then puncture his body, so they could pour poison into it. He was even allowed to walk about a bit until his legs felt heavy, leaden. Hemlock does that, gradually disable or paralyse the central nervous system.

Anyhow, I did everything normally, and, as I said, once or twice a year I oversaw the special one upstairs. It was nothing like what you hear in the newspapers nowadays. I was just another medic who became part of the justice system. These days, when I see headlines on the telly or on the Internet, it doesn't affect me the way it affects other people. I'm not shocked. Some days, I think that back then I did a bit of extra work as a medical examiner, like you have people in many countries, in your adopted country, for instance.

You were growing up, and I was growing our money.

I was one of the senior doctors at the hospital, as I

said. I want to tell you, Sara, that I remained a calm and composed man for the next ten years or so. Resigned to the loss of Atiya and distance from you, yes, but I learnt to be satisfied and grateful. As I grew older, I saw things from a different perspective. I often remembered Abbu's dictum that there exist things in the world and the hereafter that become comprehensible only with age and experience. 'Yes, we know you're good at arithmetic and biology and physics, kids, but don't you forget for a second that you need your mother and father to help you understand the world,' he'd say if Shabi and I ever said 'I know'.

~

Atiya's loss was a wound I didn't try to heal. It was best left open. I didn't change a thing in our bedroom or in her cupboard. Her clothes stayed in the same position as she'd left them. Her comb, her make-up kit, her large brush—she didn't like little nifty hairbrushes—even some of her hair stayed on the dresser. Of course I dusted the area every now and then. But no one ever slept in her place, no one.

Of course, I still have some of her things, Sara. I'd like you to keep them after I'm gone. Inside my bedroom cupboard, you will find a wooden locker, it's not locked. If you want to see them, take them, they're all in there.

The monthly report from your school was the one thing I looked forward to most. From report to report, from class to class, from group photo to group photo, that's how I counted and expended time. You were getting bigger and

I was growing older, and I thought it's fine, we're alright, we'll survive Atiya's loss.

My decision to remain where I was had paid off. That's what mattered, and everything else—my work, my compromises, my ... solitary life—was secondary. My decision to work hard and earn as much money as possible was the right one, and you know what gave me unquestionable proof of it? You, my dear, you were, are, the living proof of it.

~

And soon, Sara—I've wanted to tell you this for the longest time—I stopped doing the other thing! I stopped completely. Let's say after about ten or eleven years, give or take, I stopped. I simply ended it. The workshop carried on, obviously, but I stopped going there altogether.

I lived over there for nearly another decade, as I said, until I was absolutely certain that I'd taken care of you, your future, and there was nothing at all that could go wrong on your front. It was that simple.

I stopped, and no one said a word.

Sir Farhad remained unchanged in his manner with me, and never brought up the matter. He just let me be and do my job. I was now the Deputy Medical Superintendent of Accident & Emergency at his hospital, making a lot more money than we needed, so I saved and saved, month after month, year after year. It helped that I had no taxes to pay.

28

I KNOW I'VE BEEN A bit, how do I describe it, meandering, Sara, circling around. In my defence, I did promise myself that I'll tell you everything, the whole truth, and I didn't want Biju's shenanigans, if I may call it that, to take over.

You know, Urdu has perhaps the finest word for autobiography. Two words, as a matter of fact. *Savanah-e-Umri*—the occurrences or accidents of one's life, literally. I like it over everything else. Isn't it wonderful? Isn't that what really happens to us all, occurrence, accident?

Anyhow, as you know, Biju was always a very competent man. He knew his work so well that he could do it with his eyes closed. Not that there was too much to do. After he'd called me names and quarrelled with me over, well, over nothing and everything basically, I kept a certain distance, as I said. I didn't stop talking to him. Rather, being the sort of friends we were, I just made sure I didn't fall for his provocations. And to be fair to him, I think he also curbed his brusque side. I had a job to do, responsibilities to fulfil, staff to look after, sometimes even assist with procuring supplies and, of course, I had finances and audit to deal with ... He had none of these responsibilities and I think it suited him. I know it did.

'A free bird even if short-lived. That is how I've lived and how I'll continue to live my life, Kaiser Mian. I want to be the bird that soars high in the sky, all alone, with you all, the whole world, below me. There's nothing more precious, but you won't understand it,' he said to me a few months before his departure. I'd always found it amusing when Biju resorted to using Muslim forms of greeting to display his progressive and secular credentials.

I understand, sir, I understand very well. You see, that was one of Bij's bigger flaws. He was convinced that what he knew or understood about life and the world was imperceptible to everyone else around him.

~

He still teases me sometimes. In the email he sent last year, Biju said, 'Yes, Dr K, just come over. It'll be enormous fun meeting after such a long time, boss. God's Own Hand in God's Own Land.' He's always been fond of quips, but I'm certain he was doing it deliberately. This man who's lounging it up in his restaurant and health resort, some traditional healing bunkum in Kerala, sending me emails when I least expect them.

I'm not sure if I can say this to her, but sometimes, in my sleepless hours, I wonder if maybe it was always him. Sara last came to visit years ago. She was a teenager then—can you believe that, a teenager? Since then she's been extremely busy, as I said. Crucial years at the university, work experience, internships, high-profile job, trips across America and what not! I pray she doesn't have to take those horrible red-eye flights they have in the US of A. (Life used to be so much simpler in my time.) It all adds up, makes sense, doesn't it, if I think about it that way—and yet, I've waited and waited. It's my daughter I'm talking about. If Atiya was around, she would get it instantly, but then if she was here, perhaps I, we, wouldn't be where we are.

Anyhow, Biju's first ever email came around the same time, probably a few months after her last visit. A fifteen-year-old girl she was then! And she hasn't come since then. Yes, that's right. Curse this damn e-mail world. God only knows what all he's told her. I'd just finished setting up this place, last touches and all. Out of nowhere one day, Biju appeared in my Hotmail. At first, as I read the 'Subject', I thought it was a mistake:

Salaams & Hellos from Kerala
Remember me, Dr K, your old friend, Bij? I hope you do, boss, but no worries if you don't, because I remember you well, sir, very well. I hope you're well and not grown too fat in your post-retirement life. Btw, how's your wonderful daughter. Sara? God bless her.

If you're wondering how I found your email address, then you've probably forgotten that I was the one who helped you set it up. On the supercomputer they gave you, your blue iMac, boss, remember?

Anyhow, I felt we should stay in touch, and thanks to technology, we can now reconnect with old friends wherever they are, correct? What do you say, boss?

Convey my love to baby Sara.
Yours truly,
Biju

I froze, I didn't respond, and I didn't access my Hotmail for weeks. Then I logged in and read his email again.

Now, each time he writes, I pretend civility and old friendship. What else can I do? I think he too feigns let bygones-be-bygones while, I suspect, his real intent is to pester me. To remind me forever, to never let me forget, to keep dragging me back to the past.

~

I'll also tell Sara that most others have disappeared from my memory, faded away. They were nameless entities anyway, bodies we had to do things to in accordance with the law of the land. Many faded away sometime after the initial break.

I remember Rosie of the childlike wrists. Of course I remember her and her grateful bright smile. And the father and son, tied to one another forever the day they were reduced to halves, yes, I remember them too. Then there was the poet or soothsayer or raconteur of ancient epics. Oh yes, I remember his tapestried crimson back, but most others, almost all, really, I don't remember much, apart from the fleeting, unnerving half-glimpse of a face that suddenly returns from years ago. Back then, I'd also see a face hover briefly in the night air before me. Thankfully, thank god, the dream with the hands didn't last too long.

But my friend remains, inviting me to his fucking holiday resort or bar in Kerala.

~

So, you see, there's one reminder of those days, one witness who remains and taunts me with his name. With his existence. And that person is Biju T. Tharakan. I've felt over the years that the longest relationship I've had in my life has been with him. He's always there, somewhere in my head, lurking, smiling, nodding. I can feel and smell his breath sometimes, or maybe that's just my head. He's the source of my perennial discomfort with memory, and I don't like it. I mean, I know how to keep it in check, but he pops up suddenly. Typical, isn't it? He used to pop up suddenly even then, land at our door on a weeknight and say, 'What's for dinner, Babi?' I don't remember a single time when Atiya sent him back without feeding him a huge meal. Oh, my dear, his appetite was legendary, wasn't it? I suppose it was surprising, probably also mildly funny, because he was such a trim and fit man. Have I told you what Atiya said about him once? Where does he keep all the food, Kaiser, where does it all go, into a well? Oh, yes, I've told you...

~

You know, Sara, one of the few things I've learnt in life is that no one dies without regrets. Every person takes some, perhaps many, regrets with him or her. There's no point fretting over settling scores, tying up loose threads, aiming for closure, getting back at someone, or apologising for every little thing. Yes, as my mother used to say, a good human being shouldn't do anything that he regrets the next morning. I tried to live by this motto, even as it became abundantly clear that it's just not possible to live a regret-free life. To the grave it'll all go anyway, but one must try, one must try.

~

Biju wasn't really a drunkard, after all. He wasn't a bad person either. You and I both know that. Atiya, of course, knew it better than anyone else did—she wouldn't have been kind to him, fed him, asked me time and again to be good to him if he hadn't been a good man. Period. My preconceptions, many of which were unknown even to me, may have got the better of me. At the time, I really didn't know and I'm truly sorry.

My wise mother also used to say that no upbringing is worse than being brought up on a daily diet of prejudice. It darkens the soul permanently.

With Biju, I realised this later, much later. That I may have judged him harshly, that I may have let my *subliminal* prejudices, if I may, get the better of my rational self sometimes. That I'd allowed superstition to cloud reason.

You see, growing up in Saharanpur, I often heard it said in the house or in the neighbourhood that Sardars and Mallus are inveterate drunks. 'The drinking man will sell his wife's jewellery, or steal his child's school fees for alcohol, that's what alcohol does to you,' Abbu said almost every time I'd been out with my friends at night. I didn't even know where or how to buy alcohol, for god's sake. You remember Aapa, Ammi's aunt who used to tell us scary folk tales? She had a few drunken Sardars in her tales too. They may have been legends and horror stories about the Partition, added to, transformed over the decades, I figured as I grew up. Abbu, may god bless his soul and may he rest in eternal peace, probably disliked the drunken man more than a murderer. He was an educated man and yet he held some, how shall I say it ... not very pleasant views about other people. On matters of hygiene, for instance, it was impossible to dissuade my great father from the notion that Hindus and Christians are impure. 'They eat everything, halal, haram, jhatka, clean, unclean and they all drink alcohol—hence proved!' he shouted at Shabi, as she tried to reason with him one weekend. She'd just turned twenty, and wanted to go to a party with her friends Tabu, Zehra and Prerna. I'd long given up arguing with Abbu over such matters.

~

Anyhow, as it happened, Biju wasn't exactly what I thought he had become. He certainly loved his drink but he was not a drunk. For many years, I didn't know the difference between the two. I'm sure you can understand, Sara. He loved to eat, but he was not a glutton. He loved such things as freedom of choice, free will and the rights of the individual, even if just in theory, but he was not self-obsessed or selfish.

Maybe it was all in my head, maybe even the smell I'd smell on him, as we'd wait for coffee at Zoheb's, was in my head. Maybe some of the hurtful things he said to me weren't all that hurtful, after all. Maybe I judged him in the same manner as he judged me. Maybe Biju was and is just a classic fun-loving person, a hedonist, and because for him having a good time involved drinking, I thought he wasn't a man of character.

These things have rolled and churned in my head for so long that they don't distress me any more, certainly not as much as they bothered me when it first struck me that I may have been wrong on occasion. I've come to own them, you see. And Biju remains a presence, like a landmark of shame. This I perhaps dislike the most, and yet, and yet, I can't disentangle myself from the sole witness of my days and nights in those days.

The past, Sara, isn't a snake that sneaks up on you from the bush. For me, the past is more like an essential and immortal parasite that lives off me, boring away bit by bit. I'm aware of it all the time. Of its constant scratch and pluck, damn it. Of its corrosive little canines. One day, it will have eaten me all, consumed me whole. And then I will die. But death doesn't scare me, I think of it all the time, *almost* all the time, but it doesn't frighten me. It's fine, really, it's no big deal.

I do, however, regret and mourn the fact that this is who I'm going to die as, if you know what I mean. I can't do anything about that—can I?—because nothing can be done about it…

~

Anyhow, you know, when I said I just stopped one day and no one said a word, do you know what had happened? I stopped attending to penal cases after a decade or so, and no one said anything.

~

Dear Father,

I came to London and I haven't been since ... I know. You know.

It was the first time I properly and fully understood what had become of you: I saw a shining shell in place of my father. I saw a pretend man in place of my dad.

When I talked to you, it was as if I was talking through you, my words sinking without sound, not getting anywhere. I remember every moment. That's the curse and blessing and fucking pain of having a sound memory. But unlike that poet, I cannot beseech God to snatch my power of recollection. Because no matter what the cost, no matter what the fucking toll, I want to know and remember everything.

I came to London and you wanted me to go to the London Eye.

I came to you and you wanted to know if I wanted to eat the legendary saag gosht at Sardar's of Covent Garden or the lamb chops at Khan's of Kingsway, or if I'd prefer this new thing called Strada on the Southbank!

I came and you wanted to know if I wanted to get my hair done at Harrods. I know, Dad, it was all love and care and all that, but...

I came to London and you wanted to know if I wanted to shop at Selfridge's or at Burberry. I didn't like Selfridge's, it smelled of cabbage and perfume and leather.

You wanted to know if I needed new travel cases. Then insisted I carry those hideous stainless steel-tipped ones from some exorbitant shop in

Knightsbridge because they were burglar-proof and literally unbreakable.

You wanted to know what chocolates I liked. Not every girl likes chocolates, father.

You wanted to know if I wanted to go to Windermere for a weekend. I came and you wanted to take me on a boat trip on the Thames: all the way to the Prime meridian, you said.

I came to you and you wanted to show me the sights and scenes of London. The tower! The fucking tower of London, and that awful, awful, place, Madame Tussauds, where some necrophiliac capitalist makes money from showing us dead and alive people as they would look if they were made of wax. The idea of standing next to a smudgy, badly painted wax version of Mother Teresa or fucking Amitabh Bachchan repulsed me. What kind of people queue up for hours so they can take a photo with a weird wax statue that may or may not resemble a famous or infamous person? Madonna made of wax! Why the hell? Madge is alive. She sings. She's fucking awesome, and I can see her in countless videos on YouTube, but my father wants to know if I want to see a pale, candle-shit Madonna of Baker Street.

I am sorry, Dad.

I came to you, and you were worried if I wanted to see London. To go to the West End and Oxford Circus and Brick Lane and Liberty and the Kew Gardens (which I love, by the way, please don't get me wrong, and the West End and the British Museum too!).

No, Dad. No.

I wanted to live with you, spend time with you,

listen to you and look at your face, you silly, silly man. I wanted us to heal. I wanted your daughter to inhabit the same space as you, father.

I wanted us to sit next to each other to close the separation of years. I wanted us to remember Mummy, to tell one another her stories. I wanted to hear you talk about the amazing Atiya Hussain. I wanted to share in your memory of her, and I wanted to see her when she was a young woman, when she met you and you her.

I wanted us to sit together, with each other, not put presents and John Lewis between us.

I wanted to try and lift the darkness from your face so I could see my father.

And yes, of course, I wanted you to talk about those days when you did what you did. But above everything, I wanted to ask: why the hell did you send me away? How dare you? What kind of filial love involves putting your daughter in boarding school in another country soon after her mother dies! Yes, I'm going to say this, write this, again and again for all the years I haven't said it.

~

Let me explain what I meant by the whispers I heard. It's time. They were whispers about my father.

Whispers not among strangers but between my very own: between Uncle Aqil and Auntie Zaynab.

I was visiting one long weekend, with nothing much to do except eating desi food, the main incentive for me to visit during term breaks. Not that I had a lot of choice in the matter.

I was twelve and a few months, with Potter No. 5 in my hand probably. Loafing around the house, I drifted into the kitchen. Across the door from it was their home theatre, where they often watched Indian films, or one of those never-ending, cross-generation, sexist family sagas. As I put the book down on the counter to get some juice from the fridge, I heard the name 'Kaiser' through the door. Uncle Aqil's voice. Then hush-hush. Then 'Atiya'. Auntie Zaynab's voice. Then I heard 'silly'. Uncle Aqil. Unclear in relation to whom: my father, my mother, *me*? I froze and felt like dying. Then some more words (I wish that door had never existed.): 'Father', 'us', 'we', 'girl', 'America', 'we', 'poor' and 'careful.' I heard 'Kaiser' one more time, and then, with something like a block of ice on my chest, I left.

Nothing can be more piercing for a young girl than hearing someone talk about your father or mother in low voices, with a side eye on you probably. You know they're talking about your dad; you know they don't want you to hear it; you know they've taken your father or mother's name. You want to scream: what the hell are you saying about my mum and dad? How fucking dare you! At the same time, a part of you doesn't want to know in case it's something you cannot hear, something you cannot bear.

But even worse is the suspiciousness it engenders. You hear some murmurs again someday, and you try not to think of them. You tell yourself it's something else, because it can be anything, and yet a worm writhes in your mind.

I have thought about that day ever since.

Whispers about my father. You don't know what it does to you.

Ought I to feel shame?

Was I supposed to be ashamed of my father?

I wanted to come and tell you it's kinda all right, Dad, it wasn't entirely your fault or doing, and that you are not a bad man. Never were. Why didn't you come clean to me? Why did I have to make do with the whispers?

You're a man who did it and a man who didn't do it. You're someone whose soul met a life-changing accident. That's how I have thought of you sometimes. Please forgive me.

I wanted to mourn what happened to us, to you, to me, to Mummy. I wanted to tell you that the world is complicated and warped, and that billions of men have lived and died and each one of them has done or has had to do things they'd be more than happy to erase from the slate, wholly undo them: reset time. I wanted to be your consolation.

I wanted you to cry tears of regret, Dad, and ask me to come back. I wanted you to want me back. Did you never want me back? Why? Why never?

Then I went back to America. To college. To university. Into a big world of kind and unkind strangers. And I spent the next decade or so trying to make sense of it all: of what you sometimes did for a few years as part of your work (is that the sum of it?), why you did it and of what happened to you.

You are my father. You loved me more than anyone else in the world, in some ways more than my mother did. Yet, you kept us apart, on either side of a hellish gulf that should have never been born.

I wished you would take my hand and pull me back across the oceans. What grief, pain or darkness lay there that couldn't be overcome with me holding your hand.

Why did you not send for me? Your offspring and progeny, your mirror-form? Why didn't you come to get me? I waited all those years, more than ten years, for you to come and get me. In that time, I went from teenage to youth to womanhood, father.

Did you not believe yourself when you said that I was the best of you and Mom? That I was beyond anything you'd imagined. Did you not say that when I was small?

How did it come to this, then, that you did not need me? Or is it that daughters are not supposed to have the kind of shoulder a father may sometimes need?

Now I'm fine where I am and I'm fine with what I have done with my life, however brutal it's been, but I miss the life I could've lived with you.

If, like Ammi, you didn't exist in physical form, I'd be fine with that too: my parents died when I was very young. I could've harnessed the pathos of an orphaned childhood, and at least explained life to myself in those terms—death and loss and fate and God—if not create a story of solace for myself.

But all these years you exist in your frigging exclusive penthouse by the river. How could I not think of you? Of you and me.

Perhaps you don't understand, or perhaps you do: for me, you existed more and became more the moment Mum ceased to be. You became a double parent, a parent combined, an everything parent, all-in-one, the day we put my mother under that heap of soil.

You loomed large then, Dad, as my shelter and guardian. I wanted to hug you twice every time I hugged you. You became a giant, and I was relieved, happy, that you became so instantly.

Then you diminished the giant, not abruptly, not immediately, but slowly, year by year, cheque by cheque. You did not come.

And I did not understand it. Why the management? Isn't that what you and Uncle Aqil decided to do many years ago, when your wife and his sister died: *manage* me? Why the strangeness! Was I not familial, dear, enough to be shown closeness?

Or did you think me weak? Did you decide when I was little that I was going to be a weak person? Or did you think I was extraordinarily strong, so I'd be okay, able to withstand anything and everything? Or did you wrench me away from yourself so that I would become strong? Because you feared if I had my father's boundless love I'd grow up to be a weak and unfit person? I do not understand any of it, father.

When I saw you in London, I sensed that you

were going to turn yourself into a wreck of gloom, but that you'd call me, or come to me, if it got too tough, because I was now old enough to understand and feel.

Then I went back to the third phase of my cancerous life.

~

Sometimes, when my gaze is off the page, I admire the colours of the train: grey, steel, blue, metal, zinc or oxygen colours, colours of resilient solids. Sky, ocean, earth, all mixed up.

~

I will be honest, Dad, and I'll speak with love, for I have loved you in the only way known to me. Like a little girl.

You are a good man, a very good man: that's the reason you became a perfect wreck. You are, certainly were, a great father. A good man, a good father. But not good enough.

You're a man who did it and a man who didn't do it. You are a man whose soul was wounded in an accident. I wrote that earlier, I know. It's taken me more than a decade to think of those words, and that's how I have thought of you since.

~

I have some of Mummy's things. You gave them to me when you saw me last. On some days, I spread her things on my bed, a comb, a silk scarf, two night hair-bands, the gold necklace with its tiny ruby, her reading glasses, a few hairclips, one of them broken, and I touch them. I run my palm and fingers over them. Then I look at them standing up or sitting on the edge of the bed, depending on the light of the day. Sometimes they evoke her presence, an obscure presence, but one I can feel. You know the feeling you have when you enter a room someone's just been in, or when someone has crossed your path whilst leaving? You almost expect to see them, or some form of them, in the room. That kind of presence. I'm grateful for it. At other times, I feel nothing. Her things fail. It's been so long.

It's tough to fully conserve the memory of a face, even when they are your mother and father. I wanted to, and I could have added to her image through you, you telling me about her, mum via dad. But that was not to be.

It's been more than a decade since I saw you, and I don't know when I'm going to be able to snap out of our cycles of separation. But what I do know is that the price of your professional misstep, or what you chose to do, shouldn't have been me. Your agony might have been less if I hadn't been cast away.

You were not a bad man, father.

Do you remember how you slept with me on our armchair because you didn't want Ammi to lose any sleep? You'd have to go to work the next morning, to the hospital, but you insisted on putting me to sleep.

I've spent all my life asking myself what made such a man remove himself from the embrace of his daughter. I have some idea about what you might say if such a question was put to you.

That it was your job, the kind of job, blah-blah, the penal work you did on the side, what you got sucked into or think you got sucked into, and the toll it took on you. That you never wanted it to take the same toll on me.

You silly, self-absorbed man, did it never occur to you that, had we been together, maybe you wouldn't have too much cause to suffer in the first place? That maybe life would've been altogether different?

I'm never going to be able to say, oh, it was nothing, Dad, forget it and move on.

Of course you did it, even if never by your hand, even if it was not for long, and you did give it up. You made decisions, and decisions involve volition. An exercise of the will. Acting upon the will of the mind. And on all those counts, you are as culpable as any man living or dead, now or in history. In the dark days of yore, or amid the silicon sparkle of our modern times.

Where I live, by the way, is the place that invented the death injection, Dad, but you already know that. If you look at the punishment map of America, you will see that almost all of it is a dark red, the colour representing the states that use the needle to cause instant death. Someone apparently invented a machine to do the job, but you know what? It still needs two people to press buttons on a console connected to a computer. Like PlayStation.

I must close the letter soon. We will be in New York in a bit. Fifty-one hours it takes, and it's now been forty-five or so.

The train I take sometimes catches enormous

speed. I like it a lot. I didn't know why for a long time, but now I do. When it takes off and runs and runs, I feel a lightness that comes with the end or suspension of responsibility. In its speedier moments, it feels as if the world outside doesn't have anything to do with me.

It screeches and steams ahead, as if it's going to escape gravity, the pull and tug of us all. I feel I am the train when that happens, that the world can't do anything to me, not get a hand on me!

For these two or three days, when I'm sliding away, I feel with my entire self, in all my selves, tangible, describable. I can see all of me. In my present and in all my history. I feel I can preserve all memory. A mnemonic conservationist.

And it's perhaps for this reason, most probably for this reason, that I found the voice to speak to you. And I want to tell you this: maybe I ought to be ashamed of my father. But I'm not. I checked and I'm not. How does one live while being ashamed of their father as he lives!

You are my father and I have decided to listen to you. And I will consider what you have to say.

29

BIJU WAS CAUGHT STEALING. Biju the anaesthetist had stolen from the A&E stores. I tried everything, but all they said was that Biju had been stealing drugs from the drugs store. Being the resident anaesthetist, he'd always had a set of keys, just in case.

It was strange, shocking, baffling, to say the very least.

Why would he steal drugs? Why would he steal anything? He just wasn't the kind.

Yes, he used to drink frequently, as often as he could slip out, or as often as his friends in admin let him slip out. And yes, towards the end, he drank more often, and I suspect, more than before, and as a result, I assumed, he'd sometimes, how do I say it... misbehave ... with me and Zoheb. But drugs? No. I refused to believe it. My friend wasn't a thief.

And yet, that little germ of doubt, of suspicion, upset me at night. What if he had really taken the drugs? For his own use. But there was no way to find out.

Ask him? No way.

It was the Chief Secretary who testified that Mr Biju T Tharakan, from Kerala, India, an employee bound by contracts to the hospital, had taken sedatives, anaesthetics, painkillers and tranquilisers from the store, and that he'd kept some of the stash in his locker. That he'd been taking things for a while, but the authorities had caught him now.

'Biju T. Tharakan. Anaesthetist, Emergency, is hereby suspended with immediate effect and till further notice.'

When I read this on the notice board and in the despatch from admin that came on Monday, it felt both like an elaborate joke, and later, as if a dear one had died, or was about to die.

Why would he steal? Why would a reasonably well-paid doctor, who was good at his work, feel compelled to rob his employers? They never said. As far as I knew, Biju didn't use drugs. Would he even know how to use A&E meds as recreational drugs, for god's sake? And it was impossible that he'd been selling them. He could be irreverent, harsh and downright irresponsible sometimes, but he wasn't suicidal.

~

It happened so suddenly, Sara, so quickly, that we had very little time. By the time I heard the full story, I mean, whatever little Zoheb and I could piece together, he was already at Corrections.

~

I ran to the Chief Secretary and demanded answers. I wasn't going to be afraid of him. To his credit, though, he listened patiently, offered me saffron tea and water, and said, Dr K, you of all people should know it's not in my hands. The law is the law and it's the same for everyone. I can't do anything. What will the other staff think if we make an exception for your friend? And if word gets out, there'll be an outcry, Dr K. Sir Farhad can't have that. I'm sure you understand.

I was in a state of shock. Whatever resentments or frictions existed between Biju and me were another matter; I just couldn't believe my friend, crazy little Bij, was locked up at Corrections. In some cell on his own, probably dreaming of good food and good wine and beer, or whatever he preferred to drink. What would he eat over there? How would the other detainees treat him? I felt sad for him.

And why on earth would he steal drugs? I couldn't believe it, and it drove me mad. As far as I knew, he had enough money, and he didn't have any responsibilities back home; he took pride in being a 'zero-responsibilities' man, 'a free bird'. Biju spent money on food and drink, food and drink, that's all. Why would he steal? But they wouldn't divulge any details. Just that one line: caught stealing drugs, Biju was caught stealing drugs, I heard all the time. It felt as if the building, the walls, the wards, the Emergency, the admin block, the hallways, the elevators ... had all decided to echo that one line.

I missed Atiya. She would've given me sane advice, and most probably shown us a way out too. But then again, I was relieved she wasn't around. She would've been heartbroken to hear what Biju appeared to have done. That he was a drug addict, as the rumour went.

—

Two weeks later, they said the Department of Justice were ready to declare a verdict. I was certain that he'd be proven innocent and let go. It was surely some misunderstanding or, at worst, a false case. There was no way my friend could've possibly done something so stupid.

Zoheb, who Biju hadn't always treated kindly, set aside his bitterness and stood by me. We talked about things we'd do together once Biju was out. I imagined the moment he'd get out of Corrections. Tired, with a fully-grown beard, perhaps even a wiser man, like in old films, you know. We'd, of course, be there to receive him. For moral support and to make him feel like a VIP, I decided to ask Jan and the others in maintenance to join us when the time came.

What's all this drama, K? Biju would surely ask. And I'd say, 'This, my dear friend, is the reception party for a very important prisoner, what else?' We'd then all go to Canal Side and buy him the best supper of his life. Yes, that would make him happy, I thought, and waited for judgement day.

~

When we found out that it was the Great Judge who'd preside over the hearing, I was relieved. A senior judge such as him, a preeminent jurist, Sir Farhad's esteemed colleague and the supreme authority on matters of jurisprudence and law, would throw the case out.

Before I move on, Sara, I must tell you that more than a few times I suspected it might have been Sir Farhad's

Chief Secretary, who, incensed that Biju had gone over his head and given bribes to a few staffers in admin, somehow had these charges concocted against Biju.

Or maybe it was for something else altogether. In the hearts of men rest both sincere affections and visceral resentments. You see, I couldn't have been the only person who knew of Biju's drinking sojourns. What if many in the hospital knew too, didn't like it, hated him for it, in fact, and in order to teach him a lesson, to make an example of him, they conspired to brand him a thief? It wouldn't be too hard, would it?

What if the Chief Secretary really was behind it all? Biju and he had never really got along. As a matter of fact, Biju didn't like him at all, and I suspect, and now I'd more reason to believe so, that the secretary always hated Biju's guts. I knew for a fact that Biju never showed Farhad's chief minion any deference. 'He's nothing more than the big boss's servile shadow, K, and in any case he's not our boss.'

What if the secretary put out the story: since the only person apart from the supervisor and the stores in-charge who had access to a range of drugs was the Emergency anaesthetist, it's clear he must have stolen the expensive meds. It's impossible that the other two would steal, he might have argued.

It was all conjecture on my part but in the absence of any information from the ... authorities, Zoheb and I came up with quite a few theories.

What more is there to know, Dr K, the Chief Secretary said to me when I tried to confront him again.

Do you not believe in our justice system, in our jurisprudence? Do you question it, doc? I don't think you want to do that. Do you think Sir Farhad and the Great Judge will allow any kind of injustice here? Do you think they'll do any wrong? I'm sure you aren't trying to suggest that your understanding of justice is better? Or are you, Dr K? If they say your friend is guilty, then he's guilty.

Of course not, sir. I don't think Sir Farhad and the Great Judge will allow a miscarriage of justice. Not at all. I'm only asking if you can help. You're, after all, a senior figure in the hospital. I apologise if my tone was harsh or if I said too much. I am sorry. I felt if there's anyone in this hospital who can help Mr Biju, it is you. He's my friend, after all, sir.

I know, I know. Look, if there was anything I could do, I would've done it by now. This is a matter of law, above my pay grade. There's nothing I can do. And why are you so worried, Dr K? If you say he's innocent, then you should have complete faith in the system.

I didn't try to persuade him after that. It wasn't up to him to decide Biju's fate, anyway.

~

How was I to find out anything with certainty, Sara, how, you tell me? You have to understand that the penal system over there was different. And no one else was too bothered, trust me. Yes, most people in the hospital expressed surprise, some sorrow too, but not one was keen to do anything about it. Hamad said, 'Just let it be, man, let it be. It's not our business and if your friend's done no wrong, God's always just, man'.

Yes, I'll come to that too. Of course, I talked to Sir Farhad, why wouldn't I.

There was no way he would allow one of his doctors to be treated in this manner. He would definitely intervene. And surely, the Great Judge would dismiss the outrageous charges and order Biju's immediate release. What a cock-up, I said to myself, what a farce, but I thought it's still best to talk to Farhad. I wasn't going to watch while Biju was being punished for some misunderstanding or because of some grudge the Chief Secretary or someone else held against him.

30

It's sufficiently clear that I can't intervene and I'm sure you'll understand.

Yes, doctor, precisely because I happen to be the director of the hospital, I can't be seen as partial. Moreover, I can't interfere in the Great Judge's work, can I? He'll do the same as he does with every case: treat it strictly in accordance with the law. And if you ask for my advice, I'd say you should have a little more faith. If your friend's done no wrong, then we have nothing to worry about and if he's guilty, then I'd rather he's sentenced properly, like anyone else would be. You are a learned man, Dr K, I'm sure you don't expect us to show him any preferential treatment. Or do you?

'No, sir', is all I could say, Sara. What else could I have said?

Let me ask you something, and I'm going to be completely honest with you, one hundred per cent honest, and I expect you to do the same.

I'll speak freely and I'd like it very much if you'll too. That seems fair to me, doesn't it?

So please tell me, is it true that your friend's sometimes been negligent at work? I've had reports that sometimes he's not fully there or that he's late, or not very attentive, so I'd be grateful if you tell me what you know.

No, sir, that's just not possible. I know Biju very well. He's a very competent, intelligent and conscientious man. He'd never neglect his work, sir, never.

Alright, Dr K, alright, I hear what you say. I believe what you say. Tell me something else, then. Does your friend drink a lot? Is it true that on occasion he's been found under the influence during working hours? Now, as I told you earlier, I'm being completely honest when I say all this has nothing to do with the case. That's for the Great Judge to adjudicate. I ask because it would help me know more about your friend's character. What sort of a man is Mr Biju, after all? What kind of character does he possess, you see...? Is there any truth whatsoever to the rumours? As you can imagine, my friend, barring a few notable exceptions, I don't find the time or the opportunity to know every member of my staff. So I urge you to be completely open with me. This has absolutely nothing to do with the case. You are both from India and I have always felt that you are a fine judge of people. It might, therefore, help us, and him, if you tell me everything.

Quite suddenly, Sir Farhad's office felt like an airless little room. The ceiling seemed to narrow down on my forehead. What could I say?

Sir, as a matter of fact, to tell you the truth, I don't remember Biju ever being 'under the influence' at work. I've seen him at work, sir, and he's always been absolutely fine, a proper, thorough professional. Definitely not the kind of doctor who'd take his job so lightly.

But he does drink?

Erm…Yes. He does. Occasionally. But I've never raised it with him, sir; it's his personal matter, isn't it? I'm sure you'd agree, sir.

What else could have I said, Sara?

What might have been a good response? I have no idea. What else could I have done? The strangest thing was, I didn't know either way. I had to speak the truth. I might have tried but I just couldn't bring myself to tell a complete lie. I didn't have the courage.

Seated in front of my boss and great benefactor, there hung a moment or two of silence between us. I felt needle pricks on my body.

If you have to go back to work, please do go ahead, I don't need to detain you any longer. Thank you for being honest with me, he said and stood up.

As I left his office, I thought not of what Sir Farhad had asked me and what I'd said to him but whether maybe, maybe, Biju had, in fact, been stealing anaesthetics for himself. Just to throw some disorder into an orderly world of rules and regulations. An act of rebellion of some sort, you know; an insane way of defying authority, I agree, but something my friend might have been capable of. A silly, self-destructive hero, like in old films, you know, those who'll do anything to challenge the system.

I also remembered that when I was in medical college—you say 'med school' in the US, don't you?—we'd sometimes hear of this racket or that in the attached tertiary-care hospital. Apparently, some rich boys drove to the hospital in the middle of the night in their four-wheel-drive jeeps to buy drugs from a contact in the hospital. It was something so far removed from my world, so weird and filmy, that nearly everyone I knew either paid scant attention to it or simply dismissed it as untrue. Even if such a thing were true, it wasn't our concern at all; my friends and I were just not into this kind of stuff. In our town, the children of the rich did all kinds of things, including having brainy students sit in exams on their behalf. Midnight drug deals at the hospital could be true or, equally, a total rumour, a tall tale spun by students who knew neither legal nor illegal drugs.

In any case, if there really had been someone in the college hospital who made money by selling drugs to rich kids at night, he'd be caught one day, I thought. My friends and I focused on burning the midnight oil and feeling ennobled in our scarcity, as we watched or heard of rich boys and girls going to the disco.

Was it possible that my friend was somehow caught up in a similar racket? Or, unbeknownst to me and everyone else, had he been an addict himself! It's not uncommon for anaesthetists to slip into the habit of using some of their meds for themselves. But it seemed inconceivable, and in the end I decided to forget about the rumours and the slurs and instead, do everything I could for him, and then leave it all to God Almighty.

If he had done no wrong, there was no way he'd be harmed, and if somehow he'd done something so stupid and insane, then he deserved to be locked up in Corrections. It broke my heart, nonetheless, to imagine him, one of our own, my friend, hunched over in a prison cell, eating whatever rubbish they fed the prisoners. I knew the place, my dear, I knew it. I'd been to Corrections a few times to help. I've already told you about it. Do you remember?

31

The day arrived too soon and too late. It was a torment to wait for judgement day because when it came, it brought great relief and fresh anxiety.

It was the day when everything would turn back to normal and Biju and I would resume our bickering. As he languished—that's the word used for prisoners—I'd started to miss our arguments, his barbs, and both his funny and unfunny one-liners. I'd started to miss watching him eat. I wished for him to come back and pick up from where he'd left. I decided to cook for him once again, as Atiya had done and urged me to do. A friend is a friend, Kaisu, you don't get too many chances at lasting friendship as you grow older, she'd said to me after Biju's last dinner at ours.

Sir Farhad called me to his office and said we were not to call Biju's parents in India. It's what he wishes and we have to respect his wishes. Your friend doesn't want his parents to know about it, about anything at all.

I remember thinking about it carefully, Sara. Since Biju was to be released in the next few days, it would indeed be pointless to worry his parents. I also knew Biju would turn up at work as if nothing had happened, so I didn't want to annoy him by telling him that I'd talked to his parents while he was in prison. You may say it was a mistake—I may think so too, now—but that's all hindsight, isn't it? I thought of Biju's return from Corrections as an opportunity to start over. As a chance to draw a line so that I didn't lose the one proper friend I had. I mean, I knew he'd never stop hectoring me on this and that, but we could certainly be nicer to each other after his brush with the law ... I'd also have something with which to shut him up.

The night before judgement day, I prayed for his safe and honourable return. I want you to know I prayed with all my heart.

I remembered Atiya, took her prayer mat out, and prayed for him. I asked God for forgiveness for my sins and for Biju's misdeeds if any. I asked the All Merciful for mercy. It felt good, it felt very, very good. I wanted to feel close to God and by praying I felt something.

A part of me wished for the night to never end so that I didn't have to wake up to any news the next day. That would be perfect, I said to myself, not being confronted with it at all, and it wasn't unreasonable, was it? There was no way Biju deserved to be punished, I knew he was incapable of any kind of theft, let alone theft from his employers, let alone the theft of expensive drugs.

I have to admit that the thought of running away did cross my mind that night. No, it wasn't cowardice, come on.

Clearly, I didn't run away. It's a juvenile idea, K, I thought as I lay awake in bed. I'll have to confront my choices when the verdict comes. I'll have to do what's right. It may present an ethical conundrum but I'll have to do the right thing. You're a wise, educated, fully grown-up man, Kaiser, I've no doubt you'll make the right decision, I heard Atiya say from somewhere behind the headrest. 'Duty Before Everything', I remembered, was the house motto of Atiya's quasi-regal ancestors. She had half joked about it, when I'd asked why she wanted to resume teaching.

I must have gone to sleep at some point before dawn. I remember promising myself that from now on, I'd be nicer to Biju than he'd been to me.

32

At the end, Sara, what happened was this.

The Great Judge decreed that Biju T. Tharakan of Kerala, India, was guilty of theft. He had stolen medicines from his employers, which is to say, Sir Farhad's hospital. He was to be sentenced accordingly.

Sir Farhad called me to his office to tell me in person. He felt he owed it to me. 'Dr K, your friend is, in fact, extremely lucky. If the charge had been selling or smuggling or moving drugs, which could have been the case, he'd have to pay the ultimate price.'

He lit a cigarillo, leaned back. 'It's evident that you're upset about it, and why wouldn't you be? He's your friend and a fellow countryman, after all. I'm quite sad too. Interesting character, your friend. I understand, Dr K. What you have to understand, however, is that we have to be fair and consistent. Our laws can't discriminate. The Great Judge can't do any favours to anyone, and I can't depart from our own system just because it's one of my own employees, can I? Not only do we have to dispense justice, we have to be seen as dispensing justice. Do you follow? I have to ensure that there's hundred and one per cent compliance, so that no one can turn around tomorrow and say that Farhad has double standards, or worse, that Farhad is an inept administrator. A weak and unworthy servant of the Renovation! Let me also assure you that your friend is getting off easily. If the charge was more serious, which it might have been, he'd be in far more serious trouble. Trust me. So, what I'm trying to say to you, and to Mr Biju, is that you should be relieved that he's being let off easy. Take my word for it.

I looked at his face, which was chin up, behind a veil of smoke, and said, thank you, Sir Farhad, thank you. Then, because all of a sudden I felt I might choke up or faint, I slumped down in the chair opposite him like a little boy.

When I said Biju was the braver man, I meant to say he was the greater man. I don't remember a single instance—not that he stayed long after his conviction—when he protested, let alone raised a ruckus. I don't remember a single time when he complained, even after the whole thing was over. I don't remember a single occasion when he ranted and railed, as he was often wont to do. I don't recall any occasion when he begged or grovelled. It was as though his loss had given him a new personality, new eyes, a new life. He listened more than he talked, which, trust me, for a man such as Biju was a monumental achievement. Of course, he didn't stay long enough for me to determine if it was a permanent shift of character or a momentary cessation of hostilities. I also wanted to tell you that he looked differently at me now, unless I'd started imagining things. There was, I sensed, sympathy and kindness on his face. I felt, how do I say it—and please don't mind me saying it—paternal towards him. It has nothing to do with you. There's no way I'd somehow made Biju a surrogate for my real child. Not a chance. Whatever he had done, whatever had happened to him, somehow made me feel more protective towards the annoying bastard. That's all.

~

For Sir Farhad, it was simply an administrative matter when at last I said I'd like to be excused from my duties—just this once, I added for emphasis, I don't know why. How could have I done it, Sara!

I didn't want to be the one to oversee the implementation of the Great Judge's order. I couldn't bear to be present in that place at that time. But how was I to say no to Sir Farhad? How was anyone to say no to him?

In retrospect, what saved me was the short meeting with Farhad during which I feared I might cry. Fate moves in small circles over our heads, doesn't it?

Farhad must have simply asked Abdel Hamad to be the supervisor, or Hamad, seeing an opportunity to rise in the big boss's books, offered to oversee a difficult procedure.

Later, Hamad said sorry to me. Sorry, man, I feel bad, man, but, as you well know, it's just a part of the job, man. For Hamad, I suppose it'd been a chance to step up, and he did.

~

I refused to be the doctor for Biju's case because I felt it was wrong.

What else could I have done, Sara?

But what about the ones before him? Why were they simple medical procedures, as any other, and the one with Biju something, how do I say it ... unfair? It's not as if I didn't feel anything then. Of course I did, of course I did, but I had some clarity about what I was doing. With Biju, however, I felt paralysed. Why did I feel that way? I have no answer to that, Sara, and I'm truly sorry.

What I do know for sure is that, after Biju, it wasn't the same.

33

It was something Biju did that showed me the truth. The horror. I'll tell her.

When he was leaving for the airport, he stopped by at the hospital and came forward to shake my hand. We both stared at it in silence. Then he swapped hands.

It broke my heart forever to think what I'd become, but there was nothing I could do about it any more. Was there? I've been like this ever since. Waiting to die.

All these years later, however, things have turned around a bit. Wouldn't you say? Even I didn't expect it. Not that I have any goddamn right to have anything turned around.

Biju and I have remained friends, well, sort of friends, anyway. You know, I wasn't really too keen on this email business before, but, as I said, some years ago he found my old drk_royal@hotmail account and wrote on it, sent pictures of his restaurant-cum-bar in Kochi. Since then he's invited me again and again. I have to say I didn't know how to respond at first. Then, I wrote to him saying I was thrilled to hear from him, and I'll definitely consider visiting, and if possible, I will bring Sara along too.

Shall we visit him together? He has a prosthetic hand now, he said. You don't have to worry.

I've wanted to tell Sara about it ever since that moment. As Biju got back into the car and his driver sped off for the airport, I knew, one day, I'd tell Sara everything. The whole truth.

When she comes, I'll tell her all. I don't want to pass away without giving her a full and honest account of my life. We will stand in the balcony, watch the river glide by, drink tea or wine—and I'll tell her. Everything.